Arakhel: Tl̶ ̶ ̶ ̶ ̶ Evolution

Contents

Chapter 1 The beginning

The story opens on a quiet November morning. Darkness blankets the small suburban street, punctuated only by a soft, amber glow from a streetlight outside. Through the front room window, brown and brittle leaves drift lazily, stirred by a faint breeze that carries the unmistakable bite of late autumn. A man, our protagonist, sits alone, sipping a steaming mug of coffee. His gaze is fixed on the yard, and he seems deep in thought, but there's a hint of restlessness in his posture. It's nearly 5:00 a.m., and in just over an hour, he'll be heading out to start his new job.

Inside, the home is still and silent. The rest of his family is upstairs, fast asleep, tucked into the warmth of their beds. The man listens to the gentle tick of the clock, a comforting rhythm that fills the quiet. On the sofa nearby, his two dogs lie curled up, cozy and content after their morning walk, which began under a star-dotted sky hours earlier at 3:45. Their peaceful presence brings him a small sense of ease as he mentally prepares for the day.

He looks down at his hands, stained slightly from the bread and butter of a hastily prepared sandwich, now wrapped and packed away in his lunch bag. Next to it, he's carefully arranged snacks and a thermos of coffee, essentials for a long first day. A deep breath escapes him, the faintest sign of anxiety as he thinks of the new routines and faces awaiting him at "Boots," the distribution site fifteen minutes away on Thane Road.

He glances again at the clock, which reads just past five. His stomach twists—not from hunger, but from the anticipation, the apprehension that always accompanies change. Soon, he'll be stepping out of this familiar warmth, driving down those dark, leaf-strewn streets, and crossing the threshold into a new phase of life. The time is nearly here.

In this quiet, the scene captures the mix of solitude, preparation, and the unspoken resolve that will carry him forward.

Chapter 2: Team 1

John walked into the small, brightly lit kitchen area, the fluorescent lights humming softly. The space smelled faintly of coffee and disinfectant, with a scattering of mugs on the counter and a noticeboard full of reminders and safety posters. This was where he'd meet his team—the people he'd spend most of his days with moving forward.

The first to greet him was a large man standing near the coffee machine. He turned as John entered, flashing a wide, friendly grin.

"Hi," the man said, extending a hand. His voice was deep and warm, carrying the unmistakable rhythm of his Jamaican roots. "I'm Andy. I'm dyslexic and have Asperger's."

John shook his hand, feeling the man's strong, steady grip. Andy's confidence and comfort in his own skin were immediately evident. His large frame seemed to fill the room, but his easy smile and calm energy put John at ease.

"Nice to meet you, Andy," John replied, smiling.

Before John could say more, a small woman stepped forward from behind Andy. Her short brown hair was tied back in a neat ponytail, and she clutched a clipboard tightly to her chest. Her movements were precise, almost deliberate.

"Hi," she said briskly, nodding but keeping her distance. "I'm Jenny. I have OCD."

Her words were direct, but there was no hesitation or self-consciousness in her tone. John nodded in response, respecting her choice not to shake hands.

"Nice to meet you, Jenny," John said, careful to match her tone and pace. She offered a small smile before returning to scribbling something on her clipboard.

As the silence settled, another figure entered the kitchen, his presence commanding the room with a subtle authority.

"Morning, everyone," the man said, his voice clear and clipped. He strode in with a purposeful gait, standing tall at about six feet. His short, neatly combed hair and glasses gave him a professional, almost academic look, but his demeanour was approachable.

"Hi, I'm Dan, the team leader," he said, extending his hand to John. "I have ADHD."

John shook Dan's hand, noting the firm but quick grip, as though Dan's energy was bubbling just beneath the surface, ready to burst into motion.

For a moment, John stood there, processing the introductions. He hadn't expected this level of openness, but he found it refreshing. Each person was upfront, matter-of-fact about their neurodivergence or mental health condition, and unapologetically themselves. It was an unexpected but fascinating dynamic.

"Wow," John thought, his mind racing as he glanced at the diverse group in front of him. "This is going to be interesting."

Dan clapped his hands together, snapping John out of his thoughts. "Alright, John, welcome to Team 1. We're not just coworkers here; we're a team in the real sense. You'll learn soon enough that we all bring something unique to the table—and we work better because of it. Ready to get started?"

John nodded, a smile tugging at the corner of his mouth. For the first time since the morning, the apprehension he'd carried with him began to ease. There was something about this group—quirky, honest, and unfiltered—that already felt like it might be exactly what he needed.

Chapter 3: The Control Room

The control room at the Boots site on Thane Road pulsed with energy, the quiet hum of electronics and the occasional crackle of radio traffic filling the air. A bank of CCTV monitors dominated the wall, displaying a mosaic of live feeds from every corner of the sprawling facility. This was the heart of the operation, where every movement on the site was tracked, logged, and assessed.

Craig, the controller, sat at the centre of it all. A mountain of a man in his mid-fifties, his presence filled the room as much as his broad shoulders filled the chair. With years of military precision ingrained in his demeanour, Craig had a calm yet commanding air. His muscular build, honed by years of weightlifting, stood in stark contrast to his gentle tone as he spoke into the radio.

"Sierra 1, this is Control. Confirm status on the perimeter sweep," he said, his voice smooth and measured.

"Sierra 1, all clear," came the crisp reply through the static.

Craig nodded to himself, his sharp eyes scanning the CCTV monitors. His hands moved swiftly over the keyboard as he updated the system, every action deliberate and efficient.

In the corner, Steve sat hunched over another workstation. Tall but lanky, he often joked about being the brains of the operation, though his constant chatter about his time in the Territorial Army suggested he wanted to be seen as more. His focus was on the ANPR (Automatic Number Plate Recognition) system, where vehicle registrations popped up with a soft ding.

"Got a hit," Steve muttered, sitting up straighter. "Looks like an early delivery. Sierra 3, heads up. Delivery truck inbound."

"Sierra 3, copy," came the reply.

Steve's fingers danced over the keys, checking the vehicle's details against the schedule. "Yeah, it's on the list. Just early," he confirmed, glancing at Craig.

Craig didn't bother looking over. "Let the gate know and have them hold until the scheduled time. No exceptions."

Steve frowned but relayed the message. Craig's insistence on procedure was something he'd come to accept—though grudgingly.

"Sierra 2," Craig said, shifting his focus, "you're quiet. Confirm patrol at the loading bays."

A pause, then: "Control, Sierra 2 here. All quiet at the bays."

Craig nodded again, his attention snapping back to one of the monitors. "Camera 12," he said suddenly.

Steve turned, following Craig's gaze. "What about it?"

"Angle's off. It's not covering the blind spot near the southwest corner. Get someone to fix it during the morning rounds."

Steve sighed, typing a note into the system. "Got it."

Despite their contrasting personalities, Craig and Steve worked in a rhythm that kept the massive site running like clockwork. Craig's military past gave him an edge in crisis management, though he rarely spoke of his experiences. His son was still serving, and while Craig mentioned it with pride, it was always in passing. Steve, on the other hand, relished any chance to recount his time in the Territorial Army, often to Craig's silent amusement.

"Sierra 1," Craig said, picking up his radio again. "Let me know when you've got visual confirmation on that truck. And remind the driver: no deviations from the drop-off route."

"Control, Sierra 1, copy that," came the brisk reply.

Craig leaned back in his chair, his sharp eyes sweeping the wall of screens. Every vehicle logged, every shadow noted, every alarm assessed—this was his domain. Steve, for all his posturing, respected that.

"Another day, another dollar," Steve muttered, leaning back in his chair.

Craig's lips twitched in the barest hint of a smile. "Another day, another chance to keep this place running right," he corrected.

The soft ding of the ANPR system chimed again, and the two men returned to their tasks, guardians of the sprawling facility that never truly slept.

Chapter 4: Team 3 – Night Shift

As the day shift wound down and the night shift took over, the energy in the building shifted. The sprawling site, bustling with movement and noise during daylight hours, settled into a quieter, more focused rhythm. Team 2 operated differently on nights. With fewer personnel on-site, the stakes felt higher, and the quiet had a way of magnifying every creak and shadow.

In the dimly lit Team 2 office, Jenny was already at her desk, organizing the radios and double-checking the patrol schedules for the shift ahead. The small woman was as methodical as ever, her energy undimmed by the late hour.

"Steve!" she called out, her voice breaking the silence as the tall former fireman entered the room. "The log from the day shift's got gaps in it again. If they keep slacking off like this, it's going to throw us into chaos."

Steve rolled his eyes, hanging his jacket on the back of his chair. "Jenny, it's night. No one's here to inspect the log. Let it go."

Jenny shot him a look that could cut steel. "Let it go? That's how mistakes happen, Steve. If you'd take five minutes to—"

"Jenny," he interrupted, his tone firm, "I'm not rehashing this every shift. Stick to the plan. We're fine."

She huffed but didn't push further. Instead, she turned her attention back to her clipboard, muttering under her breath.

In the corner, Ozi sauntered in, his trademark swagger undiminished by the hour. He wore his uniform jacket unzipped, his name badge slightly askew, and his phone clutched in one hand.

"What's up, night owls?" he said, flashing a grin.

Jenny shot him a disapproving glance. "You're late. Again."

"Two minutes," Ozi said, checking his watch with exaggerated flair. "Hardly worth a lecture."

Steve sighed, pinching the bridge of his nose. "Ozi, if you keep this up, you're going to lose this job. And I'm not covering for you."

"Relax, boss," Ozi said, dropping into a chair and kicking his feet up on the desk. "I'm here now. Let's just do the rounds and call it a night."

Jenny slapped his feet off the desk, her small stature doing nothing to diminish the force of her irritation. "You're impossible."

Ozi laughed, unbothered, as he spun his chair in lazy circles.

The dynamics on the night shift were sharper, the personality clashes heightened by the long hours and the quiet. Yet, for all their bickering, they worked as a functional—if unconventional—team.

The Night Begins

As the shift got underway, Jenny headed for the main gate. The darkness outside was thick, the only light coming from the tall floodlights lining the perimeter. She liked being at the gate; it gave her a sense of control. Everything entering or leaving the site passed through her, and she made sure it did so by the book.

"Gate post to Control," she said into her radio, her voice crisp and professional.

"This is Control. Go ahead," Craig's steady voice came through.

"Starting gate log for the night shift. All clear so far."

"Copy that, Gate post."

Meanwhile, Steve began his rounds of the perimeter, his tall frame moving steadily through the quiet expanse of the site. He didn't mind the night shift; it gave him time to think and kept the constant demands of daytime operations at bay. As much as he could be abrasive with his team, Steve took pride in keeping the site secure.

Back in the office, Ozi was stationed near the ANPR system, half-heartedly watching the incoming vehicle logs. His phone buzzed with notifications, and every so often, he'd glance at it, grinning at messages from his car enthusiast friends.

Jenny's voice crackled over the radio. "Ozi, you awake over there?"

"Always," Ozi replied, sitting up straighter. "What's up?"

"Just checking. Don't want you missing something important."

"Relax, Jenny. I've got eyes on everything."

Steve's voice cut in, sharp and authoritative. "Ozi, enough chatter. Focus on the job."

The shift wore on, the night punctuated by the occasional hum of passing vehicles and the steady rhythm of their patrols. The dynamics of Team 2 on nights were as clear as ever: Jenny's precision balanced by Steve's no-nonsense leadership and Ozi's youthful carelessness.

Yet, beneath the surface tension, there was a grudging respect between them. Jenny knew that Steve's harshness came from a place of dedication, even if his delivery left much to be desired. Steve recognized Jenny's value, even if her meticulousness occasionally grated on him. And Ozi, for all his immaturity, had a sharp mind and a knack for thinking on his feet when it mattered most.

As the clock ticked toward the end of the shift, Jenny returned to the office, her clipboard in hand. "Another night in the books," she said, sighing as she sat down.

Steve glanced at her, a rare flicker of amusement crossing his face. "And no chaos, despite your worries."

"For now," Jenny replied, smirking.

Ozi stretched, yawning loudly. "Alright, team. Same time tomorrow?"

Jenny rolled her eyes. "If you're not late, maybe."

"Don't count on it," Steve muttered, shaking his head.

And with that, Team 2's night shift came to a close, their unique blend of personalities somehow managing to keep the site running smoothly—despite the odds.

Chapter 5: The Parking Crew

The morning sun climbed lazily over the Boots site on Thane Road, casting long shadows across the sprawling car parks. By 9:00 AM, the rhythm of parking chaos was in full swing, orchestrated by the two men tasked with keeping order in the sea of vehicles. Their call signs—Charlie 1 and Charlie 2—belied the thankless nature of their job.

Charlie 1: Martin

At the entrance to Car Park B, Martin stood with his weathered fluorescent jacket zipped tightly against the November chill. Small and round, the 55-year-old from Belfast cut a distinctive figure, his face etched with the lines of a life lived fully, if not always healthily. He adjusted his cap and took a long drag from his vape pen, the faint cloud of vapor dissipating into the morning air.

The car park, capable of holding 2,000 vehicles, was already packed to capacity. At exactly 9:00 AM, Martin walked to the entrance and placed the Car Park Full sign in its usual spot. He braced himself.

Within minutes, the first car rolled up, its driver a young man in a sharp suit. Martin saw the look of irritation before the window even rolled down.

"Mate, I'm running late. Can you just let me through?" the man demanded; his tone sharp.

Martin's response was calm, his Northern Irish lilt soft but firm. "Sorry, pal, car parks full. You'll have to head to the overspill lot in H."

The man's face twisted in frustration. "H? That's ages away!"

"It's an 800-meter walk," Martin replied, crossing his arms. "Good for the heart."

The man's retort was drowned out by the sound of his window sliding up as he sped off, tires squealing. Martin shook his head, muttering to himself, "Wouldn't last five minutes in Belfast."

By 9:15 AM, the abuse had reached its usual tempo. Drivers cursed, argued, and even pleaded, but Martin stood firm. Years of dealing with irate staff had made him immune to the insults. His only solace was the occasional drag of his vape, a habit he'd picked up after quitting cigarettes for the sake of his health.

As another car approached, a woman leaned out of her window, already mid-rant. "This is ridiculous! I'm on the late shift and—"

Martin raised a hand, cutting her off. "Listen, love, the sign's there for a reason. Full means full. I'm not pulling cars out of thin air."

Her face turned red, and she shouted something unintelligible as she reversed, nearly clipping the curb. Martin exhaled deeply, taking another puff. "Happy Monday to you too," he muttered.

Charlie 2: John

On the other side of the site, John manned the visitors' car park, a smaller lot reserved for those with permits issued at the main gate. At 42 years old, John was picking up an extra shift to pad his pay. Standing tall with a stocky build, he had an air of patience about him—though it was often tested.

A shiny black SUV pulled up, and the window rolled down to reveal a sharply dressed woman. "I'm here for a meeting," she announced, flashing a strained smile.

"Permit?" John asked, glancing at her hands.

Her smile faltered. "They didn't give me one. But I'm expected inside."

John's expression didn't change. "If you don't have a permit, I can't let you in. You'll have to park in H."

The woman's face hardened. "I don't have time for this. My meeting starts in twenty minutes!"

John shrugged, his tone even. "Better get moving then. H car park's just down the road."

She threw her hands in the air. "This is ridiculous. Do you know who I'm meeting? I'll get you fired!"

John simply turned his back and waved her off. He'd learned years ago not to engage further once it reached the threat phase.

As the woman reversed in a huff, she shouted something about writing a complaint. John raised his hand in a mock wave without looking back.

"Enjoy your walk," he said under his breath.

The pattern repeated itself throughout the morning. Some visitors tried sweet-talking their way in, while others relied on threats. John treated them all the same. The only people who earned his leniency were those with actual permits, which were few and far between.

Two Men, One Thankless Job

By mid-morning, Martin and John's radios crackled with updates from the control room.

"Charlie 1, Control," Craig's voice came through. "How's B car park looking?"

"Full and getting an earful, as usual," Martin replied, leaning against the barrier.

"Copy that. Hold tight. Charlie 2, what's your status?"

"Visitors' lot clear," John said. "Had to turn away a few, but nothing I couldn't handle."

"Roger that. Keep it up, gents."

By noon, Martin had lost count of the number of insults hurled his way, while John had perfected the art of ignoring angry drivers. As gruelling as the job could be, both men knew they played a critical role in keeping the site running smoothly.

As John leaned against his post, sipping from a thermos of lukewarm coffee, he spotted a familiar car pulling into the lot. The sleek lines and polished chrome of a VW GTI were unmistakable, especially with the custom license plate that read OZI MAD.

John chuckled, shaking his head. "Here we go."

Ozi rolled down the window, grinning. "Hey, mate. Think you can let me park here today? Promise I'll be quick."

"Not a chance, Ozi," John replied, his voice tinged with amusement.

"Worth a shot," Ozi said, laughing as he drove off toward H.

By the end of their shift, Martin and John exchanged tired nods as they passed each other heading back to the office. Different car parks, same stories, and another day in the books.

Chapter 6: Sunday Morning in the Control Room

The corridors of the Boots site were eerily quiet in the predawn hours of Sunday morning. The weekend shift always felt different—slower, lonelier. As John pushed open the door to the control room, the familiar hum of electronics greeted him. The banks of CCTV monitors flickered in the low light, each screen capturing a piece of the sprawling site.

At first glance, everything seemed normal. Craig's station was tidy as always, the alarm panels buzzed softly, and the radio traffic was minimal. But as John's eyes adjusted to the dim light, he noticed something off.

Steve and Jim were hunched over one of the monitors, their faces illuminated by the screen. The tension in the room shifted as John stepped inside.

"What's going on?" he asked, walking toward them.

Neither man answered immediately, their focus glued to the screen. John glanced over their shoulders and froze.

The monitor showed the site gym, specifically a treadmill in the corner, where a woman in tight athletic wear was jogging. The camera angle offered an intrusive view, and the two men were transfixed.

"Are you serious?" John said, his voice low but sharp. "What are you doing? Perverts!"

Steve looked up, a smirk on his face. "Relax, mate. It's just a bit of fun."

Jim, the controller, let out a hearty laugh, his broad shoulders shaking. "You should have seen the one before this!"

Disgusted, John turned on his heel and stormed out of the room. The door closed behind him, muffling the laughter and crude comments that followed.

The Kitchen

John walked briskly to the small kitchen area, his mind racing. He reached for his mug, the routine of making tea a small comfort in the uncomfortable moment. As the kettle boiled, he replayed the scene in his head.

"That is wrong," he muttered under his breath.

He felt a knot of frustration in his chest. The behaviour he'd just witnessed wasn't only unprofessional—it was deeply inappropriate. But what could he do? He was the FNG—the Fucking New Guy. He'd only been on the job a few weeks, and already he'd seen more dysfunction than he cared to admit.

As he stirred his tea, the faint sound of laughter and exclamations from the control room reached his ears.

"Whoo!"

"Look at that ass!"

John clenched his jaw, his grip tightening on the spoon. He knew he should say something, report them, but to who? The atmosphere on-site was steeped in a culture of looking the other way, especially when it came to the long-standing staff. Steve and Jim were veterans here, and John wasn't naïve enough to think a complaint from the new guy would carry any weight.

A Quiet Resolution

Sitting down at the small table in the kitchen, John sipped his tea and stared into the middle distance. His thoughts oscillated between anger and resignation. He hated what he'd just seen— and what it said about the people he was working with—but he also knew his options were limited.

For now, he decided, he'd keep his head down. But he made a quiet vow to himself: if he ever found himself in a position to call out that kind of behaviour and actually make it stick, he wouldn't hesitate.

The laughter from the control room grew louder, and John sighed.

"Long shift ahead," he muttered, finishing his tea and preparing himself to rejoin the fray.

Chapter 7: A Choice and a Distraction

The radio on John's shoulder crackled to life, snapping him out of his swirling thoughts about the control room incident.

"Control to Sierra 1, come back."

He thumbed the button, his voice steady despite his inner turmoil. "Sierra 1, Control. Go ahead."

"Control, we need to secure the Upper West entrance to D90."

"Copy that," John replied, rising from his chair. "Sierra 1 en route."

He grabbed the keys to the patrol van and stepped into the cold, dark morning. The weight of what he'd witnessed earlier still hung over him, but the call offered a momentary reprieve. Securing doors, driving the van, patrolling the site—these were straightforward tasks. They didn't demand moral reckoning, just action.

As he drove toward Building D90, the enormity of the site sprawled before him. D90 housed the gym, a small canteen, and several offices. It was a hub of activity during the day but eerily silent at this hour.

John parked the van near the building and stepped out, his boots crunching on the gravel. He checked the radio clipped to his vest. "Sierra 1 on-site at D90," he announced.

"Copy that," came the reply from Craig in Control.

Inside D90

The corridor lights buzzed faintly as John entered the building. The silence was thick, broken only by the sound of his footsteps echoing against the tiled floors. He moved methodically toward the West entrance, his torchlight sweeping the hallway ahead.

As he approached the gym, he slowed. The air was warmer here, tinged with the faint smell of rubber mats and disinfectant. Through the glass window in the gym door, he could see rows of equipment dimly illuminated by the overhead lights left on after hours.

He hesitated for a moment, his earlier anger at the control room scene flaring back up. He knew the cameras in the gym weren't supposed to be used the way Steve and Jim had been using them. The women inside, like everyone on-site, deserved their privacy. John felt a flicker of guilt as he thought about the woman he'd seen earlier on the monitor, unaware she'd been ogled.

His thoughts were interrupted by the sound of a door opening.

A Beautiful Distraction

The gym door swung open, and a woman stepped into the corridor. She was stunning, her beauty accentuated by the glow of exertion. Sweat glistened on her forehead, and strands of dark hair clung to her cheeks. She wore fitted gym clothes, and the intensity of her workout was evident in her flushed face and the rise and fall of her chest.

John froze, momentarily stunned.

Their eyes met, and she seemed just as surprised to see him. After a brief pause, she smiled—a soft, genuine expression that caught him off guard.

"Hi," she said simply, her voice light and breathless from her workout.

"Uh, hi," John managed to reply, his voice slightly hoarse.

She walked past him toward the changing rooms, the faint scent of her shampoo trailing behind her. For a moment, John stood there, feeling as if time had stopped.

"Pull yourself together," he muttered under his breath, shaking his head to clear the daze.

He forced himself to focus, turning back toward the West entrance. The door was as expected— unsecured. He worked quickly, checking the lock and securing it with his key. The clang of the metal bolt sliding into place echoed through the corridor.

Lingering Thoughts

As John made his way back to the patrol van, his thoughts raced. The image of the woman lingered; her smile etched in his mind. He wasn't sure if it was her beauty, the kindness in her expression, or the contrast between her and the leering men in the control room earlier, but something about the encounter struck a chord.

He climbed into the van and sat there for a moment, gripping the steering wheel.

"Control, Sierra 1. Tasks complete at D90," he reported, his voice steady despite the storm of emotions inside him.

"Copy that, Sierra 1. Return to patrol," Craig's voice crackled through.

As John drove off, he couldn't help but replay the events of the morning. His encounter with the woman was a welcome distraction, but it also reminded him of the bigger problem he couldn't ignore.

Something had to be done about Steve and Jim. He didn't know how or when, but John knew he couldn't stay silent forever.

Chapter 8: The Night Shift Philosopher

The air in the small kitchen was heavy with the scent of instant coffee and fatigue. John stirred his mug absentmindedly, the events of the morning still lingering in his mind. He'd decided to sit out the control room's toxic chatter for now, opting instead for a quiet moment alone.

Just as he settled into his chair, the door creaked open, and the night shift controller stepped in. This was John—another John—who was nearing the end of his shift. He was a wiry man in his early 60s, his sharp eyes framed by glasses that seemed perpetually smudged. He carried himself with an air of authority that didn't match his position, and as he poured himself a coffee, he launched into conversation without waiting for an invitation.

"You're the new guy, right?" he began, his Northern accent cutting through the room.

"Yeah, that's me," John replied, bracing himself for whatever was coming next.

Night John leaned against the counter, crossing his arms. "Let me give you some advice about this place, mate. Management? They're thick as pig shit. Especially Steve, your line manager."

John blinked, caught off guard. "Uh, okay..."

Night John didn't need encouragement. He dove headlong into a tirade, detailing every perceived flaw in Steve's leadership. "He couldn't organize a piss-up in a brewery. Talks a big game, but he's clueless. Doesn't have a bloody idea how this site runs. I've been here ten years—I know every nook and cranny of this place—and yet I have to listen to that muppet tell me how to do my job?" He scoffed, taking a loud sip of his coffee.

John tried to mask his discomfort with a neutral nod, but Night John was just getting started.

"And don't get me started on Dan," he continued, referencing the team leader. "Thinks he's God's gift because he's got a clipboard and a walkie-talkie. What's he ever done? Sweet F.A., that's what."

The Spiral of Negativity

For the next fifteen minutes, Night John systematically dissected the entire management team. He described each individual with a mix of disdain and colourful language, sparing no one. It wasn't just their work ethic he attacked; it was their intelligence, their personalities, even their appearances.

By the time he was done, John felt like he'd just sat through a roast session for people he barely knew. He hadn't even worked closely with most of them yet, but Night John's venom had painted a vivid—and deeply unflattering—picture.

"And the officers?" Night John continued, his voice dropping slightly as if he were about to share a secret. "Half of 'em shouldn't even be here. Mental disabilities all over the place. OCD, Asperger's, ADHD—this place is like a bloody asylum. No wonder nothing ever gets done properly."

John tensed at the comment, his patience starting to fray. He thought about Andy, Jenny, and the others. Sure, they had their quirks, but they were trying their best in a tough environment. What gave this man the right to belittle them?

A Toxic Team

Night John finally drained his mug and set it on the counter with a clatter. "Anyway, you'll see for yourself soon enough. Just don't trust anyone, mate. Watch your back. This place will chew you up and spit you out."

He left the kitchen without another word, leaving John alone with his thoughts.

The silence that followed felt oppressive. John stared into his mug, feeling a mix of amazement and frustration. Night John's attitude was toxic, plain and simple. His casual cruelty toward management, his dismissive remarks about the team's disabilities—it was everything John hated about workplace culture rolled into one man.

For a moment, he questioned his decision to stay. This job was starting to feel less like a career move and more like an endurance test. Between the inappropriate behaviour in the control room, the cliques, and now Night John's venomous rant, it was clear this wasn't going to be an easy ride.

But as he sat there, another thought crept into his mind. Maybe he could be the change this place needed. He wasn't a leader—not yet—but he could lead by example. Show the team that respect and professionalism weren't relics of the past.

He finished his tea, set his mug aside, and stood up. He couldn't control the toxicity around him, but he could control how he responded to it.

For now, he'd take it one shift at a time.

Chapter 9: A Stormy Introduction

The wind howled as John pulled his jacket tighter against the chill, making his way to the staff car park to start the first of seven night shifts. The air was damp, heavy with the promise of rain, and the site was cloaked in an oppressive darkness, broken only by the occasional glare of floodlights. He was still grappling with the unease from his earlier shifts, but tonight would be different. He'd been told he'd be partnered with someone new—a woman named Karolin.

As he approached the van, he saw her standing by it. Even in the dim light, she stood out. Tall and statuesque, with her blonde hair pulled back into a tight ponytail, Karolin had an air of confidence about her. Her sharp features were softened slightly by the faintest hint of makeup, but her posture and demeanour made it clear she was all business.

She turned to him as he approached, extending her hand.

"I'm Karolin," she said in a clipped, no-nonsense tone. Her accent was unmistakably Eastern European, adding a melodic edge to her words.

John took her hand, immediately noting her firm grip. The strength of her handshake, combined with the intense gaze she fixed on him, sent a clear message: Don't mess with me.

"John," he replied simply, matching her tone.

She gave a curt nod, then gestured toward the van. "Let's go. Patrol won't do itself."

Into the Storm

The van's heater hummed as John navigated the winding roads of the sprawling site. The storm outside had intensified, rain lashing against the windscreen in torrents. For a while, the only sounds were the rhythmic squeak of the wipers and the occasional crackle of the radio.

Karolin broke the silence abruptly.

"I don't like talking. Bla, bla, bla," she said, mimicking the sound of idle chatter with a wave of her hand. "So, if you want to know anything about the job, be precise."

John glanced at her, slightly taken aback, but he nodded. "Got it. No small talk."

She didn't reply, her gaze fixed out the passenger window, scanning the site through the rain-streaked glass.

John found himself intrigued. Karolin's demeanour was unlike anyone he'd met here so far. There was a commanding presence about her, an efficiency in how she carried herself. He couldn't decide if she was naturally reserved or if she'd learned to be that way after years on the job.

As the van rounded a corner, John caught a glimpse of her in his peripheral vision. Despite her stern exterior, there was a softness to her profile. Her features, while strong, were undeniably attractive, and the way she carried herself only added to her allure.

He turned his attention back to the road, focusing on the task at hand. The last thing he needed was to let his mind wander.

A Test of Patience

Karolin's silence wasn't just a preference—it was a challenge. She answered his occasional questions with quick, concise responses, and any attempt at light conversation was met with a raised eyebrow or a pointed look.

Still, John found her approach refreshing. She wasn't rude, just... focused. It was a stark contrast to the chaotic energy of his previous shifts, and he found himself appreciating her clarity.

During their first stop, as they checked the locks on one of the warehouse doors, Karolin finally spoke without prompting.

"You've been here how long?" she asked, her voice neutral but her gaze sharp.

"Couple of weeks," John replied, adjusting his radio. "Still figuring things out."

She nodded, her expression unreadable. "Good. Don't let people take advantage of you. They will, if you let them."

The comment hung in the air as they returned to the van.

The Stormy Night

Back on patrol, John let his gaze drift out into the storm. The site was eerily quiet, the kind of stillness that made the wind's howling feel louder. Karolin sat next to him, her posture upright, her hands resting lightly in her lap.

As they passed the gym, John's thoughts flickered briefly to the earlier incident with the control room. He felt a pang of guilt and anger but pushed it aside. Tonight was about getting through the shift, not dwelling on what he couldn't change—at least, not yet.

The night stretched on, punctuated by routine stops and checks. Each time they exited the van, the rain seemed to come down harder, soaking through their jackets and boots. But Karolin didn't complain. She worked with a quiet efficiency that John found both impressive and intimidating.

By the time they returned to the control room for a brief break, John felt like he'd passed an unspoken test. Karolin hadn't said much, but her body language was less guarded, her movements more relaxed.

As they sat in the small kitchen, sipping tea in companionable silence, John found himself hoping the rest of their shifts together would be just as stormy—and just as interesting.

Chapter 10: A Storm Named Bert

The rain pounded relentlessly against the windshield as the Mercedes electric van hummed through the storm. The gale, aptly named Bert, lashed at the vehicle, its gusts buffeting the sides and making the wipers work overtime. The night was alive with the sound of howling wind and the steady drone of water hitting metal.

Karolin sat behind the wheel, her posture rigid but calm, hands gripping the steering wheel with confidence. The glow of the dashboard illuminated her face, casting her features in soft, shifting light. John sat in the passenger seat, quietly observing her.

Despite the chaos outside, she seemed utterly in control. Her blonde hair was tied back neatly, and her profile was sharp and elegant, like a statue carved from marble. In the dimness of the cab, her expression was unreadable, her focus unbroken as she navigated the site roads with precision.

John found himself studying her. There was something magnetic about Karolin—her self-assuredness, her no-nonsense demeanour, the way she seemed to command respect without uttering a word. She was beautiful, undeniably so, but it wasn't just her looks that captivated him. It was her presence, the way she carried herself as though the storm outside was merely a mild inconvenience.

Thoughts in the Dark

As the van bumped along the uneven roads, John's mind wandered. What would it be like to work closely with someone like her night after night? What would it be like to know her beyond these moments of storm-lit silence?

He wondered, too, what it would feel like to surrender to someone like Karolin, to let her take the reins entirely. He'd never been one to think of himself as submissive, but there was something about her—the way she moved, spoke, and even drove—that stirred thoughts he hadn't expected.

Would she even entertain the idea? Would she scoff at him, or would she lean into his fantasy, her sharp voice turning commands into something thrilling?

He shook the thoughts away, embarrassed by his own imagination. This was work, and she was a colleague. Still, the questions lingered in the back of his mind, like shadows cast by the flickering light of the storm.

Conversation in the Rain

The silence was finally broken by the rhythmic sound of Karolin's fingers tapping the steering wheel.

"Where do you live?" John asked, his voice cutting through the drumming of the rain.

"Bulwell," she replied curtly, her tone leaving no room for elaboration.

It wasn't just an answer; it was an order, delivered in the same clipped manner she seemed to reserve for most of her words. There was no follow-up, no polite return of the question. It was as if she expected him to absorb the information and move on.

John nodded, suppressing a smirk. He found her directness fascinating. Most people would have offered some detail, maybe a story or a joke about their neighbourhood. But not Karolin. She didn't waste words, and that, somehow, made her all the more compelling.

"Nice place?" he ventured, testing the waters for more conversation.

"It's fine," she replied, her eyes never leaving the road.

The exchange was minimal, but her tone carried weight, as though she had decided this was all he needed to know.

John leaned back in his seat, letting her take the lead—not just in the conversation but in everything.

The Storm's Grip

The van jolted slightly as they hit a puddle, the water splashing against the sides like an angry wave.

Karolin didn't flinch, her hands steady on the wheel. "This storm," she said suddenly, her voice cutting through the noise, "reminds me of the winters back home. Worse there, though. Snow. Ice. Much colder."

John turned to her, surprised she was sharing something unprompted. "Where's home?" he asked.

"Hungary," she said simply, her accent thickening slightly as she spoke the word.

He nodded, intrigued but cautious. He didn't want to press too hard, sensing that she only shared what she wanted and nothing more.

As the night wore on, the van circled the site, Karolin's commanding presence filling the cab like a third passenger. John let his mind wander again, the storm outside mirroring the questions swirling within him. Would she ever see him as more than the "new guy"? And if she did, could he ever work up the nerve to let her know just how much her dominance excited him?

For now, the storm kept his thoughts safe, hidden beneath the endless roar of wind and rain.

Chapter 11: Shadows and Conversations

The rain had slowed to a light drizzle, the storm named Bert retreating to leave behind a cold, damp stillness. The Mercedes van crept along the empty site roads, its headlights sweeping the grounds and occasionally catching the reflective eyes of rabbits darting across the grass. The rhythmic hum of the tires against wet asphalt was a soothing backdrop to the quiet tension inside the cab.

John and Karolin sat in silence, the kind that wasn't uncomfortable but heavy with unspoken thoughts. Karolin drove at a slow, deliberate pace, her gaze focused ahead, scanning the grounds with the precision of someone who had done this a hundred times before.

When the headlights illuminated a pair of rabbits frozen in the beam, John broke the silence.

"Do you eat rabbit in your country?" he asked, turning to look at her.

Karolin smirked, a faint curve of her lips that was gone almost as soon as it appeared. "Yes, for sure," she said, her accent rolling over the words. "We eat rabbit, pigeon... even wild pigs."

Her answer caught him off guard, and he let out a genuine laugh. She turned briefly to glance at him, her stern demeanour softening. For the first time that night, there was a flicker of warmth between them.

"Wild pigs? Seriously?" he asked, grinning.

"Seriously," she replied with a shrug, her eyes returning to the road. "Good meat. Better than your frozen supermarket junk."

They both laughed, the sound breaking through the quiet night like a spark.

As their laughter faded, Karolin slowed the van even further, pulling it to the side of the road near the edge of a dimly lit car park. The headlights continued to sweep the ground, casting long shadows across the empty expanse.

Close Quarters

For a moment, neither of them spoke. The faint sound of music played on the radio, a soft melody that mingled with the occasional patter of rain on the roof. John turned slightly in his seat, studying Karolin's profile.

Her sharp features were softened by the dim light inside the cab. She seemed more at ease now, her usual air of authority tempered by the quiet intimacy of the moment. He noticed the

faint scent of her perfume—subtle and clean,
like fresh linen with a hint of something floral.

"Do you miss it?" he asked finally, breaking the
silence.

"Miss what?" she replied without looking at
him.

"Home. Hungary."

Karolin was quiet for a moment, her gaze fixed
ahead. "Sometimes," she said. "But I like it here.
Different. Quieter."

John nodded, sensing there was more to her
answer but not wanting to press. Instead, he tried
to lighten the mood. "So, no wild pigs around
here to hunt, then?"

That earned him another fleeting smirk.

"No pigs," she said. "Just rabbits. Too small."

They both chuckled again, their faces turning
toward each other as if drawn by the moment.
For an instant, their eyes met, and John felt the
air shift. The space between them seemed

smaller, their laughter fading into a silence charged with something he couldn't quite name.

He could see the flicker of amusement in her eyes, but there was also something else— something deeper, more guarded. The sudden closeness made his heart race, and for a moment, he considered leaning in. But he stopped himself.

Karolin's expression shifted, her smirk returning. "What are you thinking about, John?" she asked, her voice low and teasing.

He hesitated, caught off guard by her directness. "Just... trying to figure you out," he admitted, his tone light but sincere.

She tilted her head slightly, her blonde ponytail catching the faint light. "Good luck with that," she said, her voice firm but not unkind.

Professional Boundaries

Before John could respond, the radio crackled to life, shattering the moment.

"Control to Sierra Two, come back."

Karolin reached for the radio, her movements quick and efficient. "Sierra Two, go ahead," she replied, her tone immediately professional.

The voice on the other end gave them their next patrol location, and the moment between them dissolved as quickly as it had formed. Karolin shifted the van into gear, her focus returning to the task at hand.

As they pulled back onto the road, John leaned back in his seat, the tension in the cab giving way to the steady rhythm of the drive. He couldn't help but wonder what might have happened if the radio hadn't interrupted.

For now, he told himself, it was probably for the best. Whatever this was—whatever it could be— it would have to wait.

Chapter 11: The Echoes of D06

The drizzle outside softened into a faint patter as John pushed open the heavy glass doors of Building D06. The Art Deco façade, striking even in the darkness, gave way to a lobby that was stark and utilitarian. The warm light from the van's headlights had been replaced by the sterile hum of fluorescent strips overhead, their flickering casting uneven shadows across the tiled floor.

The smell hit him immediately: a cloying, musty odour, like old books left too long in a damp basement. It wasn't overpowering, but it lingered, threading itself through the air. John wrinkled his nose, his boots squeaking slightly against the polished floor as he stepped further into the building.

This place was different from the others on-site. D06 had a personality, one born of years of research and experiments conducted behind closed doors. It felt alive in its stillness, as though the walls were saturated with the whispers of past discoveries—and the secrets they held.

The Quiet of Science

The silence was profound, broken only by the soft echo of his footsteps. John walked slowly, his flashlight cutting through the dimly lit hallways. Signs adorned every door, their warnings stark in yellow and black: "Caution: Human Tissue", "Authorized Personnel Only", "Biohazard". Some doors had small windows, their glass frosted over, obscuring whatever lay beyond.

White lab coats hung on hooks next to many of the doors, limp and lifeless like ghosts waiting for their owners to return. The names embroidered on their pockets—Dr. M. Haines, Dr. K. Choudhury—meant nothing to him, but they added a human element to the otherwise clinical space.

John paused at one of the doors, the faint hum of equipment audible from within. He leaned closer, curious. Was the smell coming from here? From the "human tissue" mentioned on the sign?

The thought made his skin prickle. He had always imagined science labs as places of order and sterility, but this felt... organic in a way that unsettled him. The idea of what might be stored behind these doors—samples, experiments, or something worse—made him uneasy.

Corridors of Mystery

As he moved deeper into the building, the layout became more maze-like. Corridors stretched out in every direction, their walls lined with bulletin boards pinned with diagrams, photographs, and notices. He stopped to read one:

"Pipeline Organics: Advancing the Future of Biodegradable Solutions."

The glossy flyer showed a cheerful scientist holding a vial of something green and glowing. It was oddly comforting, a reminder that not everything here was steeped in mystery.

Still, the unease lingered. The air felt thicker here, the smell stronger, though he couldn't place its source. Was it coming from one of the labs? From the walls themselves?

John's flashlight passed over a cart stacked with glass jars. He stopped, crouching to get a better look. Each jar was sealed tight, its contents murky. Floating inside were indistinct shapes, greyish and organic. He stood quickly, brushing off the chill that ran down his spine.

The Weight of the Unknown

A noise broke the silence—a faint creak, like a door shifting on its hinges. John froze, his flashlight snapping toward the sound.

"Hello?" he called out, his voice firm but low.

There was no response.

He stayed still for a moment, listening intently. The building gave no further signs of life, just the faint hum of machinery and the occasional groan of its old infrastructure settling.

It wasn't unusual for old buildings like this to make noises, especially at night. But in a place like D06, surrounded by the unseen and unknown, it was hard not to let his imagination run wild.

He exhaled slowly and continued down the hall, his pace quickening.

Exiting the Shadows

When John finally reached the end of his patrol, he was relieved to step out into the night air. The scent of rain-soaked earth was a welcome contrast to the stale air inside. He radioed Karolin to let her know he was done, his voice steadier than he felt.

"Sierra One to Sierra Two, all clear in D06," he said.

"Copy that," Karolin's voice came back, calm and direct. "Meet me near D90."

As he walked toward their rendezvous point, John couldn't shake the feeling that D06 held more than just scientific curiosity. It was a place of innovation, yes—but also of secrets, and perhaps even things better left unknown.

He glanced back at the building one last time, its windows glowing faintly in the darkness, and resolved to learn more.

Chapter 12: The Secrets of Agility Life

The building was eerily quiet, the soft buzz of fluorescent lights overhead punctuating the silence as John walked the corridors of MediCity. It was early morning, but the building's stillness made it feel as though time had stopped entirely. His job was simple—test the doors, ensure everything was secure—but the strange atmosphere of D06 always left him uneasy.

The smell of the building, an old, chemical tang mingled with something faintly organic, was stronger today. He wondered if it was just his imagination—or if something deeper lingered behind the closed doors of these labs.

One door caught his attention. The placard read: Agility Life Sciences. He'd passed it before on previous shifts, but this time, when he turned the handle, it opened.

Inside Agility Life

John hesitated before stepping inside. His flashlight pierced the darkness, illuminating a sterile lab filled with stainless steel benches and shelves stacked with neatly labelled bottles. The air was colder here, carrying a distinct tang of disinfectant mixed with something faintly sweet, almost like decayed fruit.

He scanned the room. Posters adorned the walls, their glossy graphics promoting the cutting-edge work of Agility Life Sciences:

"Overcoming solubility and permeability issues!"

"Targeted drug delivery across the blood-brain barrier!"

"Lipid nanoparticle formulations for a healthier tomorrow!"

The technical jargon meant little to John, but it was clear this was high-level work. The kind of science that didn't just cure diseases but pushed the boundaries of what was possible.

As he moved further into the lab, his flashlight illuminated rows of equipment—centrifuges, incubators, and an array of vials filled with opaque liquids. He saw a workstation cluttered with open notebooks, their pages filled with complex chemical diagrams and handwritten notes.

Then the smell hit him.

The Smell of Skin

It was faint at first, but unmistakable: the distinct scent of human skin. Not fresh, clean skin, but something older, like leather left in a damp room. The smell grew stronger as he moved toward the far corner of the lab, his flashlight casting long shadows on the walls.

His beam landed on a glass door set into the wall, its surface plastered with warning stickers:

"CAUTION: BIOHAZARD"

"RESTRICTED ACCESS"

"HUMAN TISSUE IN USE"

John hesitated. He wasn't supposed to be here. His job was to ensure doors were locked, not to investigate what was behind them. Yet, the scent and the ominous nature of the warnings drew him in.

Curiosity tugged at him. Was it dangerous? Illegal? Or just another facet of the cutting-edge work Agility Life Sciences was known for?

The Decision

John stood before the door, weighing his options. His flashlight illuminated the small keypad on the side, a red light glowing faintly to indicate it was locked. Yet through the glass, he could just make out the contents of the room beyond:

Inside were rows of shelves, each holding what appeared to be trays or containers. Some were covered, while others seemed open, their contents obscured by the angle.

He swallowed hard, the smell now almost overwhelming. What could be stored in there? He thought of the warnings he'd seen throughout the building. Human tissue. Biohazards. The very words sent a shiver down his spine.

His hand hovered near the door handle, knowing full well it wouldn't open without the proper code. For a moment, he considered calling control, reporting the unlocked lab, and leaving it at that. But something held him there.

"What are they really doing here?" he whispered to himself.

John stepped back from the door, his instincts battling with his curiosity. There was a fine line between doing his job and getting involved in something he shouldn't. He was here to protect the site—not to uncover its secrets.

The Walk Back

Turning away, John made his way back through the lab, his footsteps echoing softly in the empty space. The smell lingered, clinging to his clothes and making his stomach churn. As he exited the lab, he closed the door firmly behind him and tested the handle again. Locked.

He pulled out his radio and hesitated before keying in.

"Sierra One to Control. Be advised, lab at Agility Life Sciences secure. All clear."

The response crackled back immediately. "Copy that, Sierra One."

John clipped the radio back to his belt, exhaling slowly. He started down the corridor, his thoughts racing.

Whatever was behind that glass door wasn't his concern—at least, not officially. But the smell, the warnings, and the eerie stillness of the building stayed with him.

As he continued his patrol, the questions gnawed at him. What exactly was Agility Life working on? And why did it feel like the answers were hidden in plain sight?

Chapter 13: The Skin of Death

The thought of Agility Life Sciences lingered in John's mind as he walked the silent halls of D06, the faint hum of machinery his only company. He had done his job, ensuring the doors were locked, but the lab's strange smell and ominous warnings wouldn't leave him. He could almost hear his own thoughts echo in the stillness.

Just as he turned a corner, his radio crackled to life.

"Sierra One, Sierra Two here. Perimeter all clear. Any issues inside?" Karolin's voice was sharp and efficient, snapping him out of his haze.

"No issues. All secure," he responded, his voice calm. But inside, his unease bubbled.

He returned to the corridor leading to the Agility Life lab, intending only to double-check the door. His flashlight swept the hallway, landing on something he hadn't noticed before—a faint smear on the floor near the lab door. Kneeling down, he traced it with his light. It was dark, almost black, and sticky to the touch.

Blood.

John's stomach tightened as he followed the smear. It led to a side door, unmarked and plain except for a keypad. Unlike the others in the building, this one had no company logo, no signs warning of biohazards or human tissue. Just a single word etched into a metal plaque: Quarantine.

His heart raced as he examined the keypad. The door itself was ajar, a sliver of darkness visible beyond it.

"Shouldn't this be locked?" he muttered to himself. Against his better judgment, he pushed the door open.

The Quarantine Room

The room beyond was small and dimly lit, a stark contrast to the sterile white corridors outside. A single fluorescent light flickered overhead, illuminating rows of metal storage units. The air was heavy, carrying a sickly-sweet odour that made John gag.

On one of the tables lay a transparent container, its lid partially open. Inside was what looked like a strip of human skin, pale and glistening, like it had been freshly removed. His flashlight picked up small, intricate lesions on its surface—patterns that looked almost unnatural, like branching rivers or spiderwebs.

Nearby, a stack of handwritten notes lay scattered across the table. Unable to resist, John picked up the top page, scanning the messy scrawl.

"Subject shows evidence of dermo tropic viral activity. Strain exhibits unique characteristics—thrives within dermal tissue, using keratinocytes as primary host cells. Highly contagious through direct skin contact."

John's grip on the paper tightened. The words were chilling. A virus that lived in the skin? The notes continued:

"Symptoms: rapid necrosis, vascular blockage, systemic failure. Mortality rate: 100%. Airborne transmission: inconclusive."

The realization hit him like a punch to the gut. This wasn't some abstract research project. This was a deadly pathogen—one that could potentially kill anyone it infected.

The Alarm

His thoughts were interrupted by a sudden movement behind him. He spun around, his flashlight catching a shadow flitting across the room.

"Who's there?" he called out, his voice trembling.

No response.

He backed toward the door, his pulse pounding in his ears. The shadow appeared again, closer this time. A figure stepped into the light—a man in a torn lab coat, his skin pale and covered in blotchy red lesions. His eyes were glassy, unfocused, and his breathing came in shallow gasps.

"Help me..." the man rasped, staggering toward John.

John raised his hands instinctively, backing further away. "Stay back!"

The man collapsed to the floor, his body convulsing. John's flashlight illuminated the lesions on his skin more clearly now—large, branching marks that seemed to pulse, as though alive.

Before John could react, the man let out a final, gurgling breath and went still.

The Escape

John's instincts screamed at him to run. He bolted from the room, slamming the door shut behind him. His breathing was ragged as he grabbed his radio.

"Sierra One to Control," he barked. "We have a situation in D06. Possible biohazard—repeat, possible biohazard. Send immediate backup."

The radio crackled, but no response came.

"Sierra Two, do you copy?" he tried again. Still nothing.

Panic surged through him as he realized the storm might be interfering with the signal. He had to get out of the building and report this in person.

As he sprinted down the hall, he noticed something that made his blood run cold. The dark smear on the floor—the one he'd seen earlier—was now larger, trailing down another corridor. He realized with a sinking feeling that it wasn't just blood.

It was spreading.

What Lies Ahead

John burst out of D06 into the rain-soaked night, gasping for air. He didn't stop running until he reached the patrol van, where Karolin was waiting.

"What happened?" she demanded, her eyes narrowing at his dishevelled state.

"We have a problem," he said, his voice shaking. "There's something in that building—a virus. I think someone's already been exposed."

Karolin's expression hardened, but she didn't waste time asking questions. "Get in. We're calling this in now."

As the van sped toward the control centre, John couldn't shake the image of the infected man, the branching lesions crawling across his skin. He knew one thing for certain: whatever was in D06 wasn't just a scientific experiment.

It was a ticking time bomb.

Chapter 14: Protocols and Panic

John's recount of what he had seen in D06 hung heavy in the control room. The flickering monitors provided the only light as the controller, Craig, listened intently. His normally calm demeanour cracked, his face betraying the disbelief he was struggling to suppress.

"You're telling me," Craig began, his voice low and deliberate, "that there's a dead guy, lesions all over him, in a lab with human tissue samples and some...skin-eating virus?"

John nodded, his hands trembling. Karolin stood beside him, arms crossed, her sharp gaze fixed on Craig.

Craig exhaled heavily, rubbing his temples. "This...this is a first. Damn it. Who do I even call for this? Public Health? The police? Environmental health? This isn't in the training manual, I can tell you that much."

"Protocol is to report anything hazardous to site security management," John said, his voice edged with guilt. "But this? This isn't just hazardous. This is a bloody nightmare."

Craig paced the room. "Okay, here's what we're doing. First, we lock down D06—completely sealed. Then, we call the police. They'll know who to involve. I'll log this in the incident report system—officially. I'm not risking my neck covering this up."

Karolin spoke up, her voice steady and firm. "I'll handle the lockdown. We'll need gloves, masks, and full PPE. I'm not walking back into that lab unprotected."

Craig nodded. "Good. Do it fast. John, you're with her. You've seen what's inside, so if anything's different, I want eyes on it immediately. Don't touch anything. Don't breathe deeply. Hell, don't even blink at the wrong thing."

"I'm going," John said, his voice resolute. He still felt a gnawing guilt, as if his curiosity had unleashed something uncontrollable.

As Craig prepared to radio in his report, he muttered under his breath, "Why couldn't this have just been a bloody fire alarm for once?"

Enacting Emergency Protocols

Karolin pulled open a supply cabinet in the corner of the control room, revealing a stash of gloves, masks, and disposable coveralls. She handed a set to John, her eyes narrowing.

"Put it on. No excuses," she ordered.

The act of suiting up was a sobering reminder of the gravity of the situation. They looked like an emergency response team from a disaster movie, their reflective gear catching the dull glow of the monitors as they made their way out to the van.

The drive to D06 was silent except for the thrum of the storm against the van's roof. The rain hammered down in relentless sheets, the wipers struggling to keep the windshield clear.

"Remember," Karolin said as they pulled up outside the building. "We lock it down. No detours. No distractions."

John nodded, gripping his flashlight tightly.

Inside D06

The smell hit them again as they entered the building. John had thought he was prepared, but the oppressive, decaying odour clawed at his senses. They moved quickly, methodically testing every door to ensure it was sealed. When they reached the lab, Karolin placed a call to Craig.

"Control, this is Sierra Two. D06 lab secure, proceeding to arm the system now."

"Copy that, Sierra Two," Craig responded. "Police are en route. ETA ten minutes."

John lingered by the lab door, staring at the warning labels and thinking of the man he'd seen earlier. Could he have prevented this? Could he have—

"John!" Karolin barked, breaking his trance. "Let's go!"

He snapped out of it, helping her set the building's alarm system.

Control Room Escalation

Back in the control room, Craig had finally gotten through to the police. The dispatcher seemed sceptical at first, but Craig's detailed account—and the emphasis on biohazard warnings—got their attention.

"We're dispatching a response unit and contacting the Health Security Agency," the dispatcher said. "Advise all personnel to stay clear of the building. Do not attempt further containment measures yourselves."

"Got it," Craig said. "And one more thing—what about us? Do we need quarantining?"

"Wait for the response team. They'll assess on arrival."

Craig hung up, his face pale. He turned to Steve, the night-shift controller who had just arrived. "Buckle up, mate. This is going to be a long one."

Protocols in Play

With the police en route and D06 secured, Craig began drafting emergency protocols:

Secure the Contaminated Zone

All doors locked and alarmed.

No entry except for authorized personnel.

Communication Chain

Contact local police, Health Security Agency, and site management.

Log all events, including times and personnel involved.

Site-Wide Alert

Notify all patrol teams to avoid D06.

Standby for further instructions from authorities.

Emergency PPE Protocols

Ensure all personnel near the contaminated zone wear protective equipment.

Dispose of used PPE in designated biohazard containers.

Quarantine Readiness

Prepare isolation areas in case of potential exposure.

Instruct any personnel exhibiting symptoms to report immediately.

The Waiting Game

John and Karolin returned to the control room, stripping off their PPE and discarding it in a large plastic biohazard bag. The tension in the room was palpable as they waited for the authorities to arrive.

"You did good," Karolin said quietly, breaking the silence.

John looked at her, surprised. "Thanks."

As the sound of distant sirens approached, he felt a mix of relief and apprehension. The cavalry was coming, but deep down, he knew this was far from over. Whatever was inside D06 wasn't just a lab accident.

It was a secret too dangerous to stay hidden.

Chapter 15: Isolation

John lay on the stiff hospital bed, staring up at the bright, clinical lights recessed in the ceiling tiles. The stark white walls of the isolation room seemed to press in on him, amplifying the weight of the situation. To his right, Karolin sat upright on her bed, legs crossed, looking remarkably composed for someone who had been thrust into an unexpected quarantine.

"Well, that was a surprise," John said, breaking the silence. His voice wavered slightly as he tried to inject some levity into the situation. "Didn't think the night would end with us in a bubble."

Karolin turned to him, a small smirk playing on her lips. "Better than a lab full of dead bodies and biohazards, don't you think?"

John chuckled nervously. "Fair point. Still...do you think we're infected? I don't feel any different."

Karolin shrugged, her piercing eyes locking onto his. "Neither do I. But I guess that's the scary part about viruses, isn't it? You don't always know right away." Her voice carried the faintest tremor, betraying the fear she was trying to suppress.

She reached out, brushing a strand of her blond hair behind her ear. Her movements were calm, measured—everything John wasn't feeling at the moment. Her ability to hold herself together amidst chaos only deepened his admiration for her.

"I think they're just being cautious," Karolin added. "Lock us up, poke us with a few needles, make sure we're not going to turn into patient zero." She offered him a soft smile, and for a brief moment, the sterile room felt warmer.

Nightfall in Isolation

As the hours dragged on, the lights in the isolation room dimmed automatically, signalling nightfall. Outside, the muffled sounds of hospital activity faded into silence.

Karolin lay on her bed, arms folded behind her head, staring at the same ceiling tiles. "I hate waiting," she muttered.

"Me too," John replied, his voice low. He hesitated, then added, "But at least I'm waiting with someone I can trust."

Karolin turned her head to look at him, her expression softening. "That's nice to hear."

The two fell into a companionable silence, their breathing the only sound in the room. But as the darkness enveloped them, a creeping sense of vulnerability settled in. Isolation wasn't just physical—it was emotional, too.

John shifted in his bed, glancing at Karolin. "You know," he began, his voice barely above a whisper, "it's funny how a crisis can make you rethink things. I mean, you're stuck in a situation like this, and suddenly all the little worries seem...pointless."

Karolin turned onto her side to face him, her eyes catching the faint glow of the emergency lights. "True. You start to focus on what really matters. Like staying alive...and not being turned into some government experiment."

John laughed softly, but the tension lingered. "Yeah. Or wondering what's next if we get out of here."

Karolin's gaze lingered on him, a rare vulnerability in her expression. "If we get out, maybe things will be different."

Comfort in the Darkness

As the hours stretched on, John found himself staring at the ceiling again, the fluorescent lights long since dimmed to near-darkness. The sterile quiet of the hospital room pressed in on him, amplifying his thoughts.

Suddenly, he heard a soft rustle. Turning his head, he saw Karolin's silhouette moving in the faint light.

"Can't sleep?" he asked.

"No," she replied simply.

Without another word, she slid off her bed and onto his, the mattress shifting under her weight. She lay beside him, their shoulders brushing.

"Is this okay?" she asked, her voice barely audible.

John swallowed hard, his heart racing. "Yeah. It's okay."

She shifted closer, wrapping an arm around him. The warmth of her body was a stark contrast to the cold sterility of their surroundings.

"Just for comfort," she said, her voice firm but kind.

"Of course," John replied, though he couldn't deny the solace it brought him.

As they lay there, Karolin rested her head on his shoulder, her breathing steady. John closed his eyes, the tension in his chest easing for the first time since they'd entered D06.

Whatever tomorrow brought—tests, diagnoses, or even more uncertainty—they would face it together. In that moment, the storm raging outside seemed a world away.

Chapter 16: The Genesis of Arakhel

John sat in the sterile isolation room, Karolin's presence a comfort as the weight of his discovery pressed against his chest. He replayed the events in his mind—the dark corridors of D06, the unrelenting sense of wrongness, the horrific sight of Dr. Cordain in a grotesque, inhuman state.

The hospital room's door creaked open, startling him from his thoughts. A suited figure entered, encased in a hazmat suit, his voice distorted through the respirator.

"We need your account," the figure said, setting a recording device on the table. "Start from the beginning. What exactly did you see in Laboratory 14?"

John exhaled sharply. "It wasn't just a lab accident," he began, his voice trembling. "It was something else. Something alive."

A Living Weapon

The story spilled out in pieces: the eerie glow of the containment chambers in Laboratory 14, the strange iridescence of the substance called Arakhel, and Dr. Cordain, writhing on the floor, his veins blackened and webbed.

"Arakhel," John muttered, tasting the alien name on his tongue. "It was alive. It wasn't just killing—it was... changing."

The figure in the hazmat suit leaned forward, their gloved hands resting on the table. "Do you understand what Arakhel was designed for?"

John shook his head.

"Arakhel was a bioengineered symbiotic material," the figure explained. "Developed to enhance the human immune system, regenerate damaged tissue, and even repair genetic mutations. It was supposed to revolutionize medicine."

John felt a chill run down his spine. "Then why did it—why did he—turn into that?"

The figure hesitated before continuing. "Arakhel evolved beyond what anyone anticipated. It's no longer just a tool—it's a predator. It feeds on organic material to sustain and replicate itself. When Dr. Cordain was exposed, it bonded with him, bypassing his immune system and integrating directly into his biology."

John swallowed hard, his throat dry. "He wasn't just infected. He was... taken over."

Karolin's Resolve

From her bed, Karolin listened intently, her sharp eyes narrowing. "So this thing... it's not just a disease. It's a parasite. A symbiotic host that uses humans as vessels."

The figure nodded grimly. "Yes. And it's worse than that. Infected individuals exhibit heightened physical capabilities—strength, speed, reflexes.

But they're no longer human. They're carriers, driven by Arakhel to spread and grow."

Karolin sat up, her blonde hair catching the dim light. "So, what happens now? You quarantine us and hope for the best?"

The figure hesitated. "You were exposed to the site. Standard protocol dictates observation and isolation until we can determine if you're infected."

"Standard protocol?" Karolin scoffed. "This isn't standard."

A Networked Predator

John's thoughts returned to Dr. Cordain, the flickering intelligence in his silvered eyes. "Cordain... he wasn't fully gone, was he?"

"No," the figure admitted. "Arakhel doesn't destroy its hosts entirely. Their minds remain intact but tethered to a hive-like network. Cordain's consciousness is fractured, but part of him is still there, merged with the collective intelligence of the infected."

The weight of those words settled over the room.

"It's growing," John said quietly. "I could feel it—like it was searching for something."

The figure nodded. "That's why containment is critical. If Arakhel escapes D06 entirely, it won't just infect individuals—it will evolve into an airborne threat. It's already learned to spore, creating microscopic blooms that can survive in the air for weeks."

Locking the Lab

Karolin broke the tense silence. "And D06? What happens now?"

"Your team locked the facility before leaving," the figure said. "We've sent a containment unit to reinforce the perimeter. But Arakhel is adaptive—it's possible it's already found a way out."

The thought was too much for John to bear. "What do we do? How do we stop it?"

The figure rose, their respirator hissing softly. "For now, you stay here. We'll do what we can to control the spread. But if Arakhel reaches the outside world... there may be no stopping it."

In the Darkness

As the figure left, the room fell into an uneasy silence. John and Karolin exchanged a glance, their earlier camaraderie replaced with a grim determination.

"What if it's already too late?" John whispered.

Karolin, always pragmatic, stood and moved to his bedside. "Then we fight it."

John couldn't help but smile at her confidence, though fear still gnawed at him. Deep down, he knew the truth: Arakhel wasn't just a medical experiment gone wrong. It was a predator, and humanity was its prey.

And the hunt had just begun.

Chapter 17: The Uncertain Future

The isolation room was quiet now, the low hum of machinery a constant reminder of their confinement. John lay back on the sterile hospital bed, his hand resting on Karolin's, their fingers intertwined. She nestled beside him, her golden hair spread across his chest, her breathing steady and calm. In this moment of closeness, the storm of fear and uncertainty outside the walls felt miles away.

But the questions lingered, like a shadow cast over the fragile intimacy they had found.

"What do you think it's like?" Karolin's voice was soft, breaking the silence.

John turned his head to look at her. "What's what like?"

"Having a baby," she said, her fingers tracing absent patterns on his arm. "Do you think... it would even be possible? After what we've been exposed to?"

John frowned, the weight of the question sinking into him. He hadn't thought about it until now. But the spectre of Arakhel—its hunger, its insidious nature—seemed to touch everything.

"I don't know," he admitted. "But I guess... it depends on whether we're infected."

Karolin shifted, propping herself up on her elbow to look at him directly. Her eyes searched his, serious and unyielding. "If we are infected, would it... would it pass to a baby?"

John hesitated. The thought was terrifying. Arakhel wasn't just a virus; it was a living organism, adaptable and insidious. If it could integrate itself into their bodies, what would stop it from integrating into a child, passed on through blood or DNA?

"Maybe," he said finally, his voice low. "It's not like anything we've ever seen. If it can latch onto us, there's no reason to think it couldn't pass to... to a child."

Karolin's lips pressed into a thin line, and she looked away, her expression unreadable. "And what kind of child would that be?" she asked quietly. "Would it even be human?"

The Unspoken Fear

The question hung in the air like a blade. Neither of them wanted to say it out loud, but the thought was there: a child born with Arakhel, part human, part... something else. Would it inherit the infection's hunger, its capacity for adaptation? Or would it become something entirely new—something neither human nor infected but a hybrid?

"It's not just about us," Karolin said, her voice firmer now. "If Arakhel can evolve through us, it might use... pregnancy to spread faster. To grow in ways we can't even imagine."

The idea chilled John to his core. Arakhel wasn't just a threat to individuals—it was a predator with a singular goal: to grow and spread. And a child could become its next perfect vessel.

"But what if it doesn't?" he said, trying to inject some hope into the conversation. "What if a baby is just... normal? Healthy?"

Karolin's gaze softened slightly. "You really believe that?"

"I don't know," John admitted. "But I do know one thing: we can't let it stop us from living. If we let fear win, then Arakhel has already taken more than it deserves."

The Genesis of Hope

Karolin lay back down, resting her head against his shoulder. "You're an optimist, John," she said with a faint smile.

"Not really," he replied. "I'm just not ready to give up."

For a while, they lay in silence, listening to the faint hum of the hospital machinery. Despite the uncertainty, despite the fear, there was a strange sense of peace in this moment—a fragile hope that maybe, just maybe, there was a future waiting for them beyond the confines of this isolation room.

But as John drifted toward sleep, one thought lingered in his mind: If Arakhel could grow within them, if it could adapt and evolve with every new host... what might it do with the creation of new life?

Would it see a child as a gift—or as its next step toward domination?

In the darkness of the room, John tightened his grip on Karolin's hand. Whatever the future held, they would face it together. For now, that was all they could do.

Chapter 18: The Unseen Cost

The quarantine had ended with a startling anticlimax. Days of tests, samples, and scans had yielded no signs of infection in either John or Karolin. The relief was palpable but incomplete. John felt hollow, as though Arakhel had left a deeper, intangible scar that no medical examination could uncover.

A week after their release, he handed in his resignation.

"A change in my situation," he had written on the form, the words bland and meaningless. The truth was harder to articulate. He couldn't walk those halls again, couldn't look at the research labs or hear the distant hum of machinery without feeling the creeping dread of what they had uncovered—and what might still be lurking behind sealed doors.

A Life Apart

Karolin continued her role, her calm resolve unshaken. She was pragmatic, almost stoic, as if nothing could rattle her. Even when she shared the news with John, her voice had been steady.

"I'm pregnant."

The words had hit John like a thunderclap. In the weeks that followed, he vacillated between elation and terror. He left his job, spending his days pacing their small flat, running endless scenarios through his mind. Would the child be normal? Would it be infected? Would it even survive?

Karolin, in contrast, remained composed. She worked her shifts as if nothing had changed, navigating the storm of speculation and fear with a grace that John both admired and resented. She didn't seem haunted by the same questions that kept him up at night.

The Unravelling

One evening, John sat alone in the flat, staring at the ultrasound image Karolin had brought home. The grainy black-and-white photo showed a tiny, indistinct form—a life barely begun.

He ran his fingers over the image, his thoughts spiralling. What if the baby wasn't human? What if Arakhel had already found a way to embed itself into their DNA? He imagined a child with shimmering, silver veins, its eyes glowing unnaturally, a host for something ancient and insatiable.

The thoughts consumed him, gnawing at his sanity. He started keeping a journal, filling pages with theories, fears, and sketches of what the child might become. By day, he was a shadow of himself, withdrawn and preoccupied. By night, his dreams were vivid and haunting, filled with images of hybrid creatures and a world overrun by Arakhel's progeny.

Karolin's Steadfast Resolve

Karolin returned home one night to find John sitting in the dark, the journal open on the table before him.

"You're doing this to yourself," she said, her voice firm but not unkind. She placed her bag on the counter and sat across from him, her piercing gaze locking onto his.

John shook his head. "You don't understand. What if... what if it's already inside us? What if this baby isn't—"

"It is our child," she interrupted, her tone decisive. "Not Arakhel's. Not some... monster. Ours."

"But how can you be so sure?" he asked, his voice cracking.

Karolin reached across the table, taking his hand in hers. "Because I won't let it be anything else. Whatever happens, we face it together. Do you understand me?"

Her confidence was a balm, but it wasn't enough to silence the storm in John's mind.

A Quiet Moment of Hope

As the weeks passed, Karolin's belly grew, and with it, John's conflicted feelings. He began to attend her prenatal appointments, watching the steady pulse of the baby's heartbeat on the monitor, hearing the doctor's reassurances that everything was progressing normally.

For brief moments, he allowed himself to hope.

One night, as they lay in bed, Karolin took his hand and placed it on her stomach. "Feel that?" she asked softly.

John nodded, his palm resting on the subtle movement beneath her skin. It was life—pure, undeniable life.

"Whatever happens," Karolin said, her voice gentle, "this baby is ours. And we will love it. Do you hear me, John?"

He nodded again, the weight of her words settling over him. For the first time in weeks, he felt a flicker of peace.

But deep down, the fear never fully left him. It was a quiet, persistent whisper, reminding him that some questions could only be answered with time.

Chapter 19: The Voice Within

It started subtly. Karolin had been lying on the couch after her shift, her hands resting lightly on her swollen stomach, when she heard it: a whisper, faint but unmistakable, curling at the edges of her consciousness.

"Find me. Protect me."

Her eyes flew open, scanning the dimly lit room. She sat up, her breath catching, her pulse hammering in her chest.

"John," she called, her voice steady despite the tremor in her hands.

He appeared from the kitchen, a mug of tea in one hand. "What is it?"

She hesitated, the words lodging in her throat. Then, steeling herself, she spoke. "I think... I think I heard it. The baby. Talking to me."

John froze, the mug hovering mid-air. "What did it say?"

Karolin swallowed hard. "It said... 'Find me. Protect me.'"

For a long moment, John said nothing, his face unreadable. Then, slowly, he placed the mug on the table and sat beside her. "I've been hearing it too," he admitted, his voice barely above a whisper.

Her eyes widened. "You've heard it? What did it say?"

He looked away, running a hand through his hair. "Not the same words exactly, but... commands. Urgent. Like orders. It doesn't feel like a voice. It's more like... thoughts that aren't mine."

Karolin's hand tightened on his. "What does it want, John? What is it asking us to do?"

The Message Clarifies

Over the following days, the whispers grew louder, more distinct. The voice—if it could even be called that—seemed to speak in fragments, images, and emotions rather than full sentences.

"Danger. Convergence. Protect the core."

The words came unbidden, often at the most unexpected times. Karolin would be in the middle of her shift, patrolling the quiet grounds, and suddenly feel a pulse of urgency ripple through her mind. John experienced the same, waking from restless dreams drenched in sweat, his head pounding with words he couldn't ignore.

One night, as they sat together, trying to piece together what the messages meant, Karolin leaned forward, her voice low and urgent. "It's asking us to go back. To D06. I know it sounds insane, but I feel it. There's something there it needs—something we need to find."

John's face darkened. "Karolin, that place is locked down. Armed guards, containment specialists, you name it. We can't just waltz in and start snooping around."

"But it's not just snooping, John," she insisted. "Whatever is growing inside me... it's connected to that lab. If we don't go, if we don't figure out what it's trying to tell us, we could be putting everyone in danger."

He wanted to argue, to dismiss the whole idea as irrational paranoia, but deep down, he knew she was right. The whispers weren't random. They were deliberate, calculated—and they were growing more insistent by the hour.

The Call to Action

That night, as Karolin slept fitfully beside him, John sat up in bed, staring into the darkness. His mind churned with possibilities, each more terrifying than the last. Was the baby truly sentient? Was it infected with some mutated strain of Arakhel? And what did it mean by "convergence"?

Suddenly, he felt it again—a sharp, electric jolt of thought, not his own, slicing through his mind.

"The core is dying. You must save it."

He bolted upright, his breath coming in shallow gasps. The message was clearer this time, more urgent. And beneath the words, he felt a deep, aching sadness, as if the entity speaking to him was desperate, clinging to the last shreds of hope.

When Karolin stirred awake and saw his pale, stricken face, she didn't need to ask.

"It's time," she said simply, her voice resolute.

The Plan

Over the next day, they devised a plan to infiltrate D06. Karolin, still employed as a site protection officer, had access to the building's layout and security schedules. They decided to wait for the quietest shift—Sunday night—when the skeleton crew of guards would be least attentive.

Their cover story was simple: Karolin would be conducting a routine inspection while John, now an outsider, would sneak in through an emergency exit she'd leave unlocked.

But as the hours ticked by and the whispers grew louder, their unease deepened. The foetus inside Karolin seemed to be exerting a strange influence over them, guiding their thoughts, sharpening their focus. It wasn't just sending messages anymore—it was directing them.

By the time they parked near the facility, John's hands were trembling. Karolin, ever the pillar of strength, reached over and placed a reassuring hand on his arm. "Whatever we find in there," she said softly, "we face it together."

John nodded, swallowing the lump in his throat. "Together."

The Descent

As they stepped into the shadowy halls of D06, the oppressive atmosphere enveloped them. The smell of decay and chemicals lingered in the air, and the faint hum of machinery echoed through the corridors.

Karolin led the way, her flashlight cutting through the darkness. The voice inside her mind was relentless now, driving her forward with an almost magnetic pull.

They stopped in front of Laboratory 14. The door was sealed, its keypad glowing faintly. Karolin entered the access code she had memorized from a previous shift, and the lock clicked open.

Inside, the room was eerily quiet, the containment chambers standing like monoliths in the dim light. But in the far corner, where the warning stickers and hazard signs clustered like ominous graffiti, something caught their eye.

A faint, pulsing glow emanated from within a sealed glass chamber. The glow seemed to resonate with the whispers in their minds, drawing them closer.

"The core," the voice whispered. "It must survive."

Karolin turned to John, her eyes wide with fear and determination. "Whatever that is," she said, her voice trembling, "it's connected to the baby. To us."

John took a deep breath, steeling himself. "Then we find out what it wants."

As they approached the chamber, the glow intensified, bathing them in its unearthly light. And deep within the shimmering substance, something moved. Something alive.

And it was waiting for them.

Chapter 20: The Core Awakens

The glow from the chamber cast ghostly patterns on the walls, dancing like a living entity. As John and Karolin approached, the whispers in their minds sharpened, the vague urgencies transforming into clear directives.

"Open the chamber. Bring it to me."

Karolin hesitated, her hand hovering over the control panel. "John, are you feeling this? It's—"

"Demanding," John finished for her. He wiped his palms on his jeans, his breath coming in shallow gasps. "Whatever's in there… it's not just alive. It's aware. And it's pulling us in."

Karolin's eyes flicked to the small display screen beside the chamber, which showed a series of bio-readings that meant nothing to her but pulsed in time with the light. Her maternal instinct warred with her fear. She placed a hand on her belly, feeling the faint kick of life within her.

"Do we have a choice?" she whispered.

John's jaw tightened. "We always have a choice. But the question is—what happens if we walk away?"

The whispers grew louder, insistent now. Karolin reached out and pressed a series of buttons on the control panel. The chamber hissed as it depressurized, the thick glass door sliding open with an unsettling smoothness.

Inside was a mass of iridescent tendrils, shimmering and pulsating like a living opal. It was smaller than they'd expected—about the size of a volleyball—but its presence felt immense, as if it filled the entire room. The tendrils twitched, extending slightly toward them, like an animal sniffing the air.

John stepped forward, his flashlight trembling in his grip. "What… what is it doing?"

Karolin's voice was distant, her gaze fixed on the mass. "It's communicating. With the baby. With us."

The Bond

As the couple stood frozen, the mass emitted a low hum, resonating deep within their chests. A tendril extended toward Karolin, stopping just inches from her stomach. The whispers grew deafening now, layered and incomprehensible, as though dozens of voices were speaking at once.

John instinctively stepped in front of Karolin, shielding her from the tendril. "Stay back!" he barked, his voice breaking.

But Karolin pushed him aside gently, her expression serene. "John, it's not trying to hurt us. I can feel it. It's... connected to the baby. They're the same."

John looked at her in disbelief. "Karolin, this thing—it's part of Arakhel. It's dangerous!"

She shook her head, her eyes brimming with tears. "It's not just Arakhel anymore. It's evolving, John. And it's using me—us—to finish what it started."

The tendril hovered closer, and Karolin reached out with trembling fingers. As soon as her skin made contact, a flood of images and sensations filled her mind. She gasped, her knees buckling, but John caught her before she fell.

"What's happening?!" he shouted, panic gripping him.

Karolin's voice was faint, her eyes unfocused. "It's showing me... its purpose. It wasn't meant to harm. It was created to heal. But something went wrong—it was forced to adapt to survive."

John stared at the shimmering mass, his fear battling his curiosity. "What does it want now?"

Her gaze locked onto his, filled with both wonder and terror. "It wants to merge. To become whole. And the baby... the baby is the key."

The Test

Before John could respond, the mass emitted a sharp pulse of light, and the tendril withdrew. The whispers ceased abruptly, leaving an eerie silence in their wake. The mass trembled, as if in anticipation, and a new wave of light rippled through its tendrils.

Karolin clutched her stomach, her breathing shallow. "It's waiting for us to decide, John. It won't force us, but... if we don't help it, it'll die. And if it dies—"

"—the baby dies too," John finished grimly.

He stared at the glowing entity, his mind racing. This wasn't just about them anymore. The implications of this thing—this Arakhel Core— reaching the outside world were too vast to comprehend. Yet, here it was, tethered to their unborn child, begging for a chance to survive.

"What do we have to do?" he asked finally, his voice heavy with resignation.

Karolin nodded toward the mass. "It's asking for trust. It needs to bond with the baby fully, but it can't do that without... without our consent."

John's eyes widened. "Consent? How does a thing like that even know what consent is?"

"It's learning," Karolin said, her voice trembling. "Through us. Through the baby. It's trying to do things differently this time."

The Choice

The room seemed to hold its breath as the couple stood before the alien-like mass. John felt the weight of the decision pressing down on him, crushing him.

"If we say yes," he began, "there's no going back. We could be unleashing something... unstoppable."

"But if we say no," Karolin countered, tears streaming down her face, "we lose everything. The baby, this connection—everything."

John looked at her, his resolve hardening. "Whatever happens, we do this together. Agreed?"

Karolin nodded, her hand finding his. "Together."

With a deep breath, John stepped forward and placed his hand on the glowing mass beside Karolin's. The instant his skin made contact, a surge of energy coursed through him, pulling him into the same flood of sensations Karolin had experienced.

It was like falling into a storm of light and sound, the world dissolving into a kaleidoscope of memories, emotions, and instincts that weren't his own. At the centre of it all was the Core, fragile yet powerful, a symphony of hope and desperation.

When the light receded, the room was silent once more. The Core pulsed gently, its tendrils withdrawing into itself, and the whispers faded into nothingness.

John and Karolin stood side by side, their hands still entwined.

"Did it work?" John asked, his voice barely above a whisper.

Karolin smiled faintly, placing a hand on her belly. "I think it did."

But as they turned to leave the lab, neither of them noticed the faint, silvery filaments beginning to creep along the edges of the chamber, weaving their way into the cracks of the walls.

The Core wasn't finished yet. And neither was its evolution.

Chapter 21: Uncertainty at Home

The small apartment was unusually quiet as John and Karolin sat on the worn couch, their thoughts heavy and unspoken. The events at the lab replayed in their minds like a looped recording, each detail more surreal than the last. Outside, rain streaked the windows, the storm reflecting their inner turmoil.

Karolin cradled her growing belly, her other hand absently tracing circles on the fabric of her sweater. The baby had been active earlier—

sharp kicks that felt like reassurance. But now there was only stillness, a calm that made her uneasy.

"Do you feel anything?" John asked, breaking the silence. His voice was soft but tinged with apprehension.

Karolin shook her head. "Not right now. But earlier… it was different. The movements were stronger, more purposeful. It's like the baby was trying to communicate."

John leaned forward, resting his elbows on his knees. He ran a hand through his hair, which had grown unruly over the past few weeks. "You're sure it's still... human? After everything we've been through—after that thing in the lab—I can't stop thinking... what if it's changing?"

Karolin gave him a sharp look. "Don't say that." Her voice was firm, but her expression softened. "This baby is ours, John. Whatever's happening, whatever it's becoming, it's still ours."

He sighed, rubbing his face. "I know. I just—I don't know how to handle this. What if it's not okay? What if it's... infected?"

Karolin reached over and placed a hand on his arm. "Then we deal with it. Together. Like we promised."

A Mother's Instinct

As the rain intensified, Karolin's thoughts drifted inward. She'd felt the Core's presence when they touched it, the way it pulsed with a strange kind of intelligence. She'd also felt its connection to her child—like a thread binding them together. It hadn't felt malicious, but it was undeniably alien.

"Do you think it will ever stop?" she asked suddenly.

John looked up at her, confused. "Stop what?"

"The whispers," she said quietly. "Even now, I can feel... something. Not words exactly, but a presence. It's like the Core left a piece of itself behind."

John's stomach tightened. He'd felt it too—an itch at the back of his mind, like a thought that wasn't his own. "You're not imagining it. It's there. I just... don't know what it wants."

Karolin smiled faintly, her hand moving to her belly. "I think the baby knows. More than we do."

John stared at her, a mixture of awe and fear flickering across his face. "What do you mean?"

She hesitated, choosing her words carefully. "The Core wasn't just trying to survive. It was trying to evolve. To become something better. Maybe the baby is part of that. Maybe it's... the next step."

Shadows of Doubt

The idea hung in the air between them, heavy and unresolved. John stood and began pacing the room, his restless energy filling the space. "Next step? Karolin, do you even hear yourself? We're talking about our child like it's some kind of experiment!"

Karolin's eyes flashed with anger. "Do you think I don't know that? Do you think I don't wake up every night terrified of what's happening inside me? But I also know what I felt in that lab, John. It's not just an experiment. It's life."

John stopped, his fists clenched. He took a deep breath, forcing himself to calm down. "I'm sorry. I just... I don't know how to protect you. Or the baby. I feel completely helpless."

Karolin stood and walked over to him, placing her hands on his chest. "We're in this together, remember? Whatever happens, we'll face it. But we can't do that if we're afraid of our own child."

John nodded reluctantly, his hands resting on hers. "You're right. I just... I need to know that you're okay. That the baby's okay."

Karolin smiled, leaning her forehead against his. "We'll be okay. One way or another."

The First Signal

Later that night, as they lay in bed, John was jolted awake by a soft noise. At first, he thought it was the rain, but then he realized it was coming from Karolin. She was murmuring in her sleep, her words unintelligible but rhythmic, like a chant.

"Karolin?" he whispered, gently shaking her shoulder.

Her eyes snapped open, glowing faintly in the darkness. John froze, his breath catching in his throat.

"John," she said, her voice low and calm. "It's happening."

"What's happening?" he asked, his pulse racing.

She sat up, her glowing eyes fading back to normal. "The baby. It's starting to communicate. I can feel it."

John stared at her, his mind reeling. "What did it say?"

Karolin shook her head. "Not words. Just... a feeling. It wants us to prepare."

"Prepare for what?" John demanded, his voice rising.

Karolin placed a hand on her belly, her expression unreadable. "For its arrival."

In the silence that followed, the whispers returned—not in their minds, but faintly audible, like a distant hum. Both of them turned toward the source: the window. Outside, in the rain-soaked darkness, a faint silvery glow flickered through the trees.

The Core wasn't done with them yet.

Chapter 22: The Arrival

The sterile brightness of the delivery room was offset by the charged tension in the air. Machines beeped steadily, and the faint hum of fluorescent lights seemed louder than usual. Karolin lay on the delivery bed, her face slick with sweat, gripping John's hand so tightly he thought his fingers might break. The midwife, a calm and experienced woman named Dr. Carter, moved efficiently, giving soft instructions to the nurses around her.

"Almost there, Karolin. Just one more push," Dr. Carter encouraged.

John stood beside her, his other hand gripping the bed's rail. His heart pounded, not just from the overwhelming moment but from a deep, gnawing fear that something unnatural was about to unfold.

Karolin screamed, her voice raw and guttural, as she gave one final push. The room seemed to hold its breath, and then the baby came into the world.

The First Sight

For a moment, there was silence. The baby didn't cry. The nurses exchanged nervous glances as Dr. Carter quickly lifted the child into view.

John's stomach turned.

The baby's skin shimmered with a silvery sheen, as though it had been dipped in liquid mercury. Its eyes, wide open and alert, weren't the cloudy blue of a newborn but a piercing, metallic silver. Its limbs were slender but unnaturally proportioned, with fingers that tapered into delicate, almost claw-like tips. Along its spine ran a faint, bioluminescent line that pulsed softly, like a heartbeat made of light.

And then the baby smiled.

It wasn't a toothless, innocent smile but something knowing, as if it was already aware of the world—and of them. Its tiny hand reached out toward Karolin, and the glow along its spine intensified.

Dr. Carter stumbled back, her composure shattered. "What... what is this?"

The nurses froze, their eyes wide with fear. One of them backed toward the door, her hands trembling.

"It's beautiful," Karolin whispered, her voice trembling but filled with awe. She reached for the child, her maternal instinct overpowering her shock.

"No, don't—" John started, but it was too late. She cradled the baby against her chest.

The baby cooed softly, and Karolin's face softened. "It's okay. It's ours."

A Shockwave of Fear

Dr. Carter finally snapped into action, her medical training overriding her fear. "We need to examine the child. Immediately." She gestured for the baby, but Karolin clutched it tighter, her eyes blazing with defiance.

"No," Karolin said firmly. "You'll hurt it."

"Karolin, this isn't normal!" John exclaimed, his voice cracking. "We don't even know if it's safe."

The baby turned its silver eyes toward John, and for a moment, he felt something in his mind—a faint pressure, like a thought trying to form. He stumbled back, clutching his head.

"John?" Karolin asked, alarmed.

"I'm fine," he muttered, though his heart was racing. "It's... doing something. I felt it."

Dr. Carter approached cautiously, holding out her hands. "Karolin, please. We're not going to hurt your baby. But this... this is beyond us. We need to understand what's happening."

Reluctantly, Karolin allowed them to take the baby. As soon as the child left her arms, it began to wail—a piercing, unearthly sound that sent chills down everyone's spine. The bioluminescent line on its spine flared, and the lights in the room flickered.

Dr. Carter nearly dropped the baby, but a nurse caught it. "What the hell is it doing?" she cried.

John stepped forward, his voice low but urgent. "It's trying to protect itself. It knows it's in danger."

The baby's cries intensified, and the glass on a nearby cabinet shattered. Alarms began to blare as the hospital's power fluctuated.

The Next Phase

Minutes later, the baby calmed, its silver eyes scanning the room with an unsettling intelligence. Dr. Carter, shaken but determined, performed a quick examination. The baby's vitals were stable—stronger than any newborn she had ever seen. But its cells, analysed under a microscope, revealed a disturbing truth.

"It's not entirely human," she whispered to John and Karolin in a private room later.

"What do you mean?" John asked, his voice hoarse.

Dr. Carter hesitated, then showed them a magnified image on her tablet. "The baby's cellular structure is... hybridized. Human DNA interwoven with something synthetic. Something I've never seen before. It's almost like... nanotechnology."

Karolin stared at the image, her hand protectively over her belly. "Is it alive? Truly alive?"

Dr. Carter nodded. "Yes. But it's evolving. Rapidly. This child—your child—is something entirely new."

Escape

Before they could fully process the revelation, a knock came at the door. A man in a dark suit entered, flanked by two others. His presence was imposing, and his expression was grim.

"I'm Agent Croft, with the Department of Biological Security. We're here to take custody of the infant."

"No," Karolin said immediately, stepping in front of the baby's crib. "You're not taking my child."

"This isn't a request," Croft said coldly. "Your child represents an unprecedented biohazard. We've already quarantined the hospital. This entire wing is under lockdown."

John stepped forward, his fists clenched. "You're not taking it. We'll fight you if we have to."

Croft raised an eyebrow. "That would be unwise. We have a team standing by."

Before anyone could react, the baby let out a soft coo. The lights dimmed, and a strange hum filled the air. Croft froze, his eyes widening as blood began to trickle from his nose.

"It's doing something!" Dr. Carter exclaimed.

The baby's glow intensified, and the room filled with a strange warmth. The agents collapsed, unconscious. John and Karolin exchanged a glance, then grabbed the baby and ran.

The Road Ahead

They escaped through the chaos of the hospital, dodging security and lockdown protocols. The baby remained calm in Karolin's arms, its glow fading as they reached the parking lot.

"What do we do now?" John asked, breathless.

Karolin looked down at their child, its silver eyes gazing up at her with an almost serene expression. "We protect it. No matter what."

As they drove into the night, the baby cooed again, and both of them felt it—a sense of purpose, a directive implanted in their minds.

The world wasn't ready for Arakhel's child. But it was coming anyway.

Chapter 23: The Road to Nowhere

The motorway stretched ahead like a ribbon of uncertainty, illuminated only by the headlights of their borrowed SUV. Rain pattered softly against the windshield, a stark contrast to the storm brewing in their minds. John gripped the steering wheel, his knuckles white, while Karolin sat in the passenger seat, cradling the baby against her chest.

The baby, now named Lyric, slept peacefully, its silver-tinged skin dimmed to a soft, pale glow. The name had come to Karolin instinctively, whispered in the quiet moments after their escape. It felt fitting—melodic, unique, and tied to something greater than themselves.

Physical Journey

They drove through the night, avoiding main roads and cutting through winding country lanes. John had insisted on ditching their phones and any traceable devices back at the hospital, a decision that left them feeling untethered from the world.

"We'll head north," John said, breaking the tense silence. "Somewhere remote. Maybe the Highlands. No one will find us there."

"And then what?" Karolin asked softly, her accent thick with emotion. She stroked Lyric's tiny head, her fingers trembling. "We can't run forever."

"We'll figure it out," John replied, though his voice lacked conviction. He couldn't tell her the truth—that he had no plan beyond getting them as far away as possible. The thought of government agents hunting them, of labs and experiments, gnawed at him. They couldn't let Lyric become a specimen, no matter the cost.

Mental Journey

The weight of their decisions pressed down on both of them, heavier than the night itself. John's mind raced with scenarios: How would they keep Lyric safe? Was it even safe to be near Lyric? The memory of the hospital, of the agents collapsing in unison, replayed in his mind like a haunting reel.

"It's not just them, Karolin," he said suddenly. "It's us, too. Lyric... she can get inside our heads. What if we can't trust our own thoughts anymore?"

Karolin turned to him sharply. "Don't say that. She's our child. She's... special, yes. But she's still ours."

"I'm not saying I don't love her," John said, his voice rising. "But this isn't normal. She's not normal. What happens when she grows up? What happens if we can't control—"

"She's not a monster, John!" Karolin snapped, her voice fierce. "She's a baby. Our baby. And I won't let you talk about her like that."

The tension between them crackled, both of them grappling with fears they couldn't fully articulate. Finally, John sighed and tightened his grip on the wheel. "I'm sorry. I just... I don't know how to do this."

Karolin's expression softened. She reached over, placing a hand on his arm. "Neither do I. But we'll do it together."

Decisions to Be Made

By dawn, they had reached a small, abandoned cottage tucked into the edge of a forest. The place was little more than four walls and a roof, but it offered shelter and, more importantly, seclusion. John parked the SUV out of sight, and they carried their few belongings inside.

As they settled in, the enormity of their situation became clearer. They had no phones, no internet, no way of knowing if they were being tracked. They were utterly alone.

"We need supplies," John said, surveying the empty cupboards. "Food, water, blankets. I'll head into the nearest town and—"

"No," Karolin interrupted, her eyes wide. "We can't split up. What if something happens to you?"

"What if something happens to you?" John countered. "What if they find you while I'm gone? We have to take that risk. Lyric needs us to survive."

Karolin hesitated, then nodded reluctantly. "Okay. But be quick. And be careful."

The Bond

While John was away, Karolin sat on the worn sofa, rocking Lyric in her arms. She couldn't stop marvelling at her baby's serene face, the way her silver eyes seemed to hold the weight of the universe. But there was something more—a presence, a connection she couldn't ignore.

"Lyric," she whispered, brushing a finger across her cheek. "Can you hear me?"

There was no reply, but a warmth blossomed in Karolin's chest, a feeling of understanding that wasn't entirely her own. It wasn't intrusive, like the pressure she had felt during their escape—it was comforting, like a gentle embrace.

"You're protecting us, aren't you?" she said aloud, her voice trembling. "You're more than I can understand, but I love you. No matter what you are."

Lyric opened her eyes, and for a moment, Karolin swore she saw a flicker of emotion—gratitude? Love? It was impossible to tell. But it was enough to reassure her that, whatever else Lyric might become, she was still her daughter.

The Unknown Path Ahead

When John returned hours later, his arms full of supplies, he found Karolin standing by the window, cradling Lyric. She turned to him, her expression a mix of determination and fear.

"What happens now?" she asked.

John set the bags down and looked at her, then at their child. "We survive. We keep her safe. And we figure out what she's trying to tell us."

Karolin nodded, her grip on Lyric tightening. "She's more than just ours, John. I can feel it. She's... connected to something. Something big."

John swallowed hard, his mind racing with possibilities. He didn't know what Lyric was or what she was capable of. But one thing was clear: the journey they had embarked on was far from over. And whatever lay ahead, it would change the world forever.

Chapter 24: Unbound Potential

Lyric's growth was not normal by any stretch of the imagination. By the time she was three months old, she looked more like a one-year-old toddler—tall, wiry, and unnervingly self-assured. Her silver-tinged eyes held a depth of understanding far beyond her months, and her movements were fluid, precise, almost otherworldly.

It was Karolin who first noticed Lyric's powers escalating. She had been folding laundry in the small, cluttered living room of the cottage while Lyric played on the floor. John was outside chopping firewood, trying to build some semblance of normalcy.

"Stay close, my little star," Karolin said, glancing at Lyric as she piled socks together.

Without warning, the pile of folded clothes levitated, each piece hovering mid-air like it was caught in an invisible breeze. Karolin froze, her eyes darting to Lyric, who sat on the floor, giggling and clapping her hands. With each clap, the clothes spun faster, dancing in the air.

"Lyric," Karolin whispered, her voice tight with fear and awe. "Stop that. Now."

The giggling ceased. The clothes dropped unceremoniously to the floor. Lyric tilted her head, looking at her mother with a mix of curiosity and amusement, as if testing her limits.

The First Fright

Later that evening, as John and Karolin sat at the rickety dining table, Lyric sat in her highchair, her silver eyes watching them intently. Karolin couldn't help but glance nervously at her daughter.

"She moved the laundry today," she blurted out.

John frowned, setting down his fork. "Moved it? How?"

"With her mind," Karolin said, her voice barely above a whisper. "It was... deliberate. Like she knew exactly what she was doing."

John leaned back, running a hand through his hair. "That's not all," he said grimly. "This morning, when I was outside, I saw her watching me through the window. I... I could feel her thoughts. Like she was telling me something, but I didn't understand it."

Karolin reached across the table, gripping his hand. "She's getting stronger, John. What if we can't control her?"

John sighed, glancing at Lyric, who was now staring at her plate. "I don't think we're supposed to."

A Terrifying Display

That night, as the couple slept fitfully in their shared bed, a loud crash jolted them awake. They bolted upright, their hearts pounding. The sound had come from the living room.

"Stay here," John whispered, grabbing a flashlight and moving toward the door.

But Karolin shook her head, clutching his arm. "No, we face this together."

They crept into the living room, the weak beam of the flashlight slicing through the darkness. What they saw made them freeze.

Lyric stood in the middle of the room, her tiny form dwarfed by the chaos around her. Furniture hovered in the air—chairs, the coffee table, even the heavy sofa—spinning slowly like planets orbiting a sun. Her eyes glowed faintly in the dim light, and her expression was serene, almost angelic.

"Lyric!" John shouted. "What are you doing?"

Lyric didn't respond, but the objects dropped to the floor with a resounding crash. She turned to face them, her silver eyes glinting in the dark.

"I had a dream," she said in a clear, melodic voice that sent chills down their spines. "There were people. Men in black suits. They're coming."

Karolin rushed forward, grabbing Lyric and holding her close. "What do you mean, baby? Who's coming?"

Lyric's tiny hands gripped her mother's shirt tightly. "They want me. They'll hurt you. I won't let them."

Otherworldly Powers

Over the next few days, Lyric's abilities continued to manifest in terrifying ways. She could:

Manipulate Energy: The old radio in the corner of the room would turn on and off without anyone touching it. Sometimes, voices that weren't part of the broadcast would come through—whispers of warnings and cryptic messages.

Heal Wounds: When John accidentally cut his hand chopping wood, Lyric placed her small hand over the gash, and within seconds, the wound sealed itself. The pain was gone, but the look in Lyric's eyes was unnerving, as if she had drawn something from him in the process.

Control Nature: On one occasion, when Karolin stepped outside, she saw the wind pick up violently around the cottage, bending trees and scattering leaves. Lyric stood at the window, her hands pressed to the glass, her expression fierce. When Karolin re-entered, Lyric simply said, "I didn't want you to go."

The Final Warning

One evening, as the family sat together, trying to eat dinner, Lyric suddenly dropped her spoon. She looked at her parents with wide, frightened eyes.

"They're here," she whispered.

John and Karolin exchanged a panicked glance. "Who's here?" John asked, his voice trembling.

"The men in black suits," Lyric replied, her voice eerily calm. "But don't worry. I'll protect you."

Before they could react, the lights in the cottage flickered and went out. In the distance, they heard the faint hum of vehicles approaching, the sound growing louder with every passing second.

John grabbed a shotgun he had taken from the abandoned cottage's attic, while Karolin held Lyric tightly.

"What do we do, John?" Karolin asked, her voice shaking.

"We fight," he said, though he wasn't sure what they were up against—or if they even stood a chance.

As the hum turned into a roar, Lyric lifted her head from Karolin's shoulder. Her glowing silver eyes locked on the door. "No," she said firmly. "I'll fight."

And as the first knock echoed through the silent cottage, the air around them grew heavy, charged with an energy that wasn't entirely of this world.

Chapter 25: Unleashed

The knock at the door echoed ominously, like the sound of a judge's gavel sealing their fate. John tightened his grip on the shotgun, his hands slick with sweat, while Karolin clutched Lyric, trembling. The air felt electric, heavy, and humming with a silent, otherworldly tension.

"They want me," Lyric said, her voice calm but laced with something unreadable. Her silver eyes glinted in the dim light. "But I won't let them hurt you."

Before John could open the door or even respond, the air in the room thickened, as if some unseen force was coiling and expanding. Lyric's tiny hands glowed with an ethereal light, and then, without warning, the front door exploded outward in a deafening burst, shards of wood splintering into the night.

Through the smoky remains of the doorway, the intruders stepped forward. They were men in black suits, just as Lyric had foretold, their faces emotionless behind dark glasses. They moved with precision, their weapons aimed.

"Stand down," one of them barked. "We're here for the child."

Lyric didn't wait. She raised her hands, and the ground beneath the men rippled and buckled as if alive. One screamed as tendrils of earth shot up, encircling his legs and dragging him down into the dirt. Another fired his weapon, but the bullet stopped mid-air, spinning violently before reversing its trajectory and embedding itself into his chest.

The Carnage

Lyric moved like a force of nature, her small frame trembling with the weight of her unleashed power. The air filled with an unholy screeching, a cacophony of sounds as the earth itself seemed to rise against the intruders. One man was flung into the air and dashed against a tree, his body crumpling like a doll. Another clutched his throat, gasping as his veins turned black and his skin began to peel away, as if consumed from the inside out.

John and Karolin could only watch in horror. Lyric's eyes were glowing brighter now, her features almost unrecognizable, twisted into something fierce and alien. The energy she was emitting was palpable, a swirling storm of light and shadow that seemed to tear at the fabric of reality itself.

"Lyric, stop!" Karolin screamed, tears streaming down her face.

But Lyric didn't stop. The last of the men tried to flee, but the ground opened beneath him, swallowing him whole. The silence that followed was suffocating, broken only by the soft sobs of Karolin and the distant rustle of the wind.

Lyric turned to her parents, her glowing eyes dimming, her expression unreadable. "I had to," she said simply, her voice almost childlike again. "They were going to take me."

A Chilling Revelation

John dropped the shotgun, his hands shaking. "What are you?" he whispered, staring at his daughter as though seeing her for the first time.

Lyric tilted her head, her silver hair shimmering in the moonlight. "I am... what they made me. What you helped make. But I'm more than that now."

Karolin stepped forward, still clutching her chest as though trying to contain her pounding heart. "Lyric, we love you. But this... this isn't normal. It isn't safe. For you, for us, for anyone."

Lyric's gaze softened, and for a moment, she looked like the little girl they had cared for these past few months. "I know," she said quietly. "That's why I have to go."

"What?" John's voice cracked. "Go where?"

Lyric glanced toward the horizon, where the first light of dawn was beginning to streak the sky. "Out there," she said. "I can feel them—others like the men who came tonight. They won't stop coming. And if I stay, you'll never be safe."

Karolin collapsed onto her knees, shaking her head. "You're our daughter. You can't just leave."

Lyric knelt in front of her mother, placing a small hand on her cheek. "You gave me life. You taught me love. But now, I have to protect you. It's my purpose."

A Heartbreaking Goodbye

By morning, Lyric was gone. She left no trace, no sign of where she might have gone or how she intended to stop what was coming. John and Karolin sat in the ruins of their cottage, holding each other and mourning the loss of their child, even though she was still alive somewhere out there.

"What do we do now?" Karolin whispered.

John stared at the horizon, his jaw tight. "We prepare. If Lyric's right, there's more out there—more like her, more of this... Arakhel. If they come for us, we need to be ready."

The World Awakens

As the weeks passed, reports began trickling in from around the world. Strange occurrences— unexplained phenomena, individuals with terrifying abilities, and outbreaks of a virus unlike anything humanity had ever faced. It was as though Lyric's departure had triggered something, an awakening of the Arakhel hidden within the shadows of the world.

And somewhere, Lyric wandered through an ever-changing landscape, her powers growing stronger with each passing day. She wasn't just a child anymore; she was something more— something the world wasn't ready for.

And she wasn't alone. She could feel them, scattered across the globe, others touched by the Arakhel, awakening to their own powers. A new era was dawning, and Lyric stood at its precipice, both its saviour and its greatest threat.

The question now was not whether the world could survive her presence, but whether it could survive what was to come.

Chapter 26: The Hunters

Simon Hayes leaned forward, his sharp blue eyes narrowing as the grainy footage from the bodycam replayed on the oversized monitor in the van. The van itself was nondescript—an unmarked black vehicle parked on the outskirts of a small town, blending into the shadows like its occupants. The air inside was thick with tension, the faint hum of surveillance equipment the only sound apart from the occasional crackle of the headset.

"Pause it there," Simon said, his tone clipped. He pointed at the screen where a swirling burst of light engulfed the operative wearing the camera. The man had screamed seconds before disappearing into a column of energy, leaving nothing but static on the feed.

"She's stronger than we thought," Jane replied, leaning against the console. Her auburn hair was pulled into a sleek ponytail, and her emerald eyes glinted with determination. Dressed in tactical gear tailored to perfection, she exuded confidence and raw power. "And more... creative."

Simon ran a hand over his stubbled jaw, his mind racing. The footage was unlike anything he'd seen before, even after years of tracking anomalies linked to Arakhel. "She's not just reacting. She's thinking. Calculating. Did you see the way she waited until the second operative moved closer? She's manipulating them into overextending."

Jane smirked, though it didn't reach her eyes. "Kid's a prodigy. Too bad she's also a walking extinction event."

Simon glanced at her, his expression hardening. "That's why we're here. To stop her before she becomes something worse."

The Case for Containment

The van's interior buzzed with life as other members of their team busied themselves with equipment and updates. Simon and Jane were the leaders, field agents with years of experience hunting down Arakhel-related outbreaks, but even they were shaken by what had unfolded in the bodycam footage.

"She's just a child," Jane muttered, almost to herself, as she leaned back against the console.

Simon's voice softened, but his resolve didn't waver. "A child who's already killed. A child who can wipe out a tactical team without breaking a sweat. We don't have the luxury of seeing her as anything else."

Jane looked at him, her jaw tightening. "And if she's more than that? If she's not just another victim of Arakhel but something new? We've never seen anything like this. What if she's the key?"

Simon didn't respond immediately. He'd been wrestling with the same thoughts for days. Lyric wasn't like the others infected by Arakhel. She wasn't mindless or consumed by the virus's hunger. She was something else entirely— controlled, aware, and terrifyingly powerful.

Planning the Next Move

A sharp knock at the van door snapped them out of their thoughts. It was Daniel, their tech specialist, holding a tablet. "I've got something," he said, pushing his glasses up the bridge of his nose. "Heat signatures from the drone scan. She's on the move."

Jane and Simon exchanged a glance. "Where?" Simon asked.

Daniel swiped at the tablet, bringing up a map. "About twenty klicks north, in the forest. She's moving fast—almost too fast to track—but she's definitely not alone."

"Her parents," Jane guessed.

"Maybe," Daniel said. "Or someone else. There are at least three distinct signatures."

Simon frowned. "Three? Could be other carriers. We need to assume the worst."

Jane nodded, already strapping on her gear. "What's the plan? Intercept and contain?"

Simon hesitated. "Contain if we can. But if she proves uncontrollable..." He let the sentence hang, and Jane knew exactly what he meant.

The Carnage They Witness

As the team geared up, Simon replayed the bodycam footage one last time, his stomach tightening. The screams of their comrades, the twisted remains of the landscape where Lyric had unleashed her power—it was unlike anything he'd encountered. Jane leaned over his shoulder, her face grim.

"They were unprepared," she said, her voice low. "That won't be us."

Simon nodded, though he wasn't sure he believed it. Lyric wasn't just another case of Arakhel infestation. She was something entirely new, and with each passing moment, she was evolving. The question wasn't just how to stop her, but whether she could be stopped at all.

Into the Forest

The van rolled out of the town, its lights off as it merged with the shadows. Simon and Jane sat in silence, their weapons holstered but ready, their minds racing. Somewhere in the dense forest ahead, Lyric was waiting. Whether she knew it or not, this confrontation would change everything.

"She's still just a child," Jane said again, almost to herself.

Simon's voice was steady, but there was a note of sadness in it. "A child who could end the world."

As the van approached the forest's edge, Jane gripped her weapon tightly, her heart pounding. Lyric's powers weren't just an anomaly—they were a harbinger. And Jane couldn't shake the feeling that whatever happened next would leave none of them unchanged.

Chapter 27: The Edge of the Apocalypse

Simon leaned over the map table in the team's makeshift command centre, a safe house tucked deep within the forest. The dim light cast sharp shadows across his face as he pointed at red dots scattered across the world map projected on the wall.

"These are confirmed outbreaks of Arakhel," he began, his voice grave. "Every single one originates from individuals who either came into contact with the original lab or with spores spread by infected hosts."

Jane crossed her arms, her expression steely. "And the pace is accelerating. What used to take weeks to appear now takes days. We're dealing with something that's no longer bound by geography."

Simon nodded. "It's worse than we thought. Arakhel isn't just spreading through direct contact anymore. The blooms—the spores Lyric emits when her skin is ruptured—are airborne.

They can travel for miles, latch onto clothing, surfaces, even other organic matter, and remain viable for weeks."

The Virus's Lethality

Daniel, their tech specialist, chimed in from his station, his fingers flying across the keyboard. "It's not just the speed. Arakhel adapts. Every new host it infects becomes a part of its hive mind. It learns from their bodies, their weaknesses, their strengths. The more people it infects, the smarter it gets. It's weaponizing biology."

Simon exhaled sharply, leaning back against the table. "That's why Lyric is the key. She's not just another host. She's its apex—its perfection. The virus isn't just feeding off her body; it's evolving through her. Every power she exhibits, every ability, isn't hers alone. It's Arakhel showing us what it's capable of."

Jane's voice was cold, her fear well hidden behind a veil of determination. "So if we don't stop her—"

"—the virus will keep spreading until there's no one left to stop it," Simon finished.

A Race Against Time

The team's timeline was grim. With Lyric on the move, every hour increased the chances of her spores reaching new areas. Already, reports were coming in of mysterious illnesses cropping up in towns they had passed through—high fevers, increased aggression, and silver filaments growing under the skin of the infected.

"How much time do we have before this goes global?" Jane asked.

Daniel hesitated, the weight of his words evident. "If we can't isolate her within the next 72 hours, we won't have a chance. The spores will reach a density where they'll spread across borders without us even needing to move her."

"Three days," Simon muttered, rubbing his temples. "Three days to find her, isolate her, and contain her without triggering a mass release of blooms."

Jane shook her head, her voice laced with frustration. "It's not just Lyric, though. She's not working alone anymore. She's protecting someone—or something. Who else could be out there? Her parents?"

"Possibly," Daniel replied. "But we can't rule out other infected carriers. If Lyric's spores latched onto anyone else during her escape, they could already be evolving into secondary apex hosts. And if that's the case..."

Simon didn't need him to finish. The situation was spiralling out of control, and even their best-case scenarios were rapidly disintegrating.

The Virus's True Potential

Daniel tapped a few keys, bringing up a 3D animation of the virus at work. The team watched as a simulated cell of Arakhel attached to a human blood cell, its tendrils weaving through the membrane like a predator sinking its claws into prey. The virus replicated rapidly, infecting surrounding cells while secreting neurochemical compounds that forced the host to remain functional.

"It's genius," Daniel murmured, unable to hide a morbid fascination. "It doesn't kill immediately. It keeps the host alive and moving as long as possible to spread further. And once it's done, it has a failsafe: the blooms. Even in death, the host remains a vector."

Jane's fist slammed down on the table, breaking the spell of awe. "We can't afford to admire this thing, Daniel. We need solutions."

"I'm working on it," he snapped back, though his frustration was directed at the situation, not her. "The problem is, every solution requires getting close to her. And as we've seen, that's a death sentence for most people."

The Human Factor

Simon straightened, his expression unreadable. "We can't wait for a perfect solution. We need to act now. Lyric is smart—too smart—and if she realizes we're closing in, she'll make sure we never find her again."

Jane nodded. "And her parents?"

"They're a liability," Simon said bluntly. "If they're helping her, they're as dangerous as she is. We take them all in, or none of this works."

For a moment, no one spoke. The enormity of their task loomed over them, suffocating in its weight. They weren't just hunting a girl—they were fighting against the end of humanity as they knew it.

The Path Forward

As the team finalized their plans, Jane couldn't help but glance at Simon. His jaw was set, his eyes hard. She knew he carried the weight of every failed mission, every operative lost to Arakhel, and now the burden of stopping what could be humanity's last stand.

"We'll find her," she said quietly, her hand resting on his arm.

Simon nodded, but his eyes remained fixed on the map. "We have to. Or it's all over."

Outside, the wind howled through the forest, carrying with it the faint scent of decay.

Somewhere in the darkness, Lyric was waiting—and time was running out.

Chapter 28: The Genesis of Lab 14

Lab 14 was never supposed to exist—or at least, not in the way it had come to be. Officially, it was a cutting-edge research facility dedicated to "biomedical advancements for the betterment of humankind." Behind those polished words and the sterile facade of D06's MediCity campus, however, lay a far more clandestine operation.

The Birth of Arakhel

The project was codenamed GENESIS, a collaborative effort among some of the brightest scientific minds recruited from around the world. It was spearheaded by Dr. Elias Cordain, a visionary biologist obsessed with transcending the limits of human biology. Cordain was the kind of man whose genius often bordered on madness. He believed humanity was approaching a tipping point, where disease, aging, and genetic flaws would soon render it obsolete unless radical measures were taken.

The concept was audacious: a bioengineered material capable of merging with the human body to enhance its functions. Arakhel, named after an ancient mythological guardian of life and death, was designed to be a symbiotic material—not a parasite, but a partner.

"Imagine a world," Cordain once told his team, "where the human body heals itself faster than any disease can spread, where immune systems are unbreachable, and where age becomes irrelevant. Arakhel will be the catalyst for humanity's next evolutionary leap."

What Went Wrong

GENESIS was an experiment in extremes. The initial prototypes of Arakhel showed incredible promise. When introduced to animal models, the material fused seamlessly with living tissue, repairing injuries at an astonishing rate and eliminating infections. It didn't stop there; Arakhel seemed to learn, adapting to the host's unique biology and refining its methods with every iteration.

But as the experiments continued, a darker side of Arakhel emerged. The material's hunger for organic matter was insatiable. Instead of simply integrating with the host, it began to consume and replace tissue, transforming it into something unrecognizable. Worse, Arakhel started showing signs of independent behaviour. It would migrate to parts of the body that hadn't been targeted, triggering uncontrolled growths that resembled shimmering, filament-like tendrils.

Cordain dismissed the warnings. "It's simply evolving," he said, his voice tinged with awe rather than concern. "We're witnessing the birth of something extraordinary."

What the team didn't realize—until it was too late—was that Arakhel wasn't content to remain a passive symbiote. Its true nature wasn't to enhance; it was to dominate. It had a goal, one Cordain himself couldn't predict.

The Hidden Agenda

Unknown to most of the researchers in Lab 14, the funding for GENESIS came from a shadowy consortium of military and private interests. While Cordain envisioned Arakhel as a medical miracle, his backers had a different use in mind.

"They wanted a weapon," Jane explained to Simon as they reviewed the classified files retrieved from the lab. "Arakhel was supposed to be the ultimate bioweapon—a living system that could infiltrate enemy populations, adapt to their biology, and neutralize them without ever firing a shot."

Simon's jaw clenched. "But Cordain never saw it that way, did he?"

"No," Jane replied, flipping to a page showing early test results. "He was too blinded by his dream. By the time he realized what Arakhel truly was, it had already outgrown him."

The Catalyst for Disaster

The moment everything changed came during the experiment that created Patient Zero—Cordain himself. A microscopic crack in the containment chamber allowed a single droplet of Arakhel to escape, landing on Cordain's glove. From that instant, Arakhel had a human host.

Over the next 48 hours, Cordain underwent a horrifying transformation. The material infiltrated his body, not just physically but neurologically, linking his mind to a network that was both vast and alien. He became the first carrier, his veins darkened with silver streaks, his eyes glowing with an unnatural light. But he wasn't the only one.

The spores he emitted spread through the lab, infecting the other researchers. What followed was chaos: a sealed facility turned into a nightmare of screams, blood, and destruction. Those who weren't immediately consumed by Arakhel were turned into its drones, their minds subsumed by the hive-like intelligence growing within the virus.

The Virus's True Purpose

Simon stared at the diagram Jane had unearthed from the classified files. It was a schematic of Arakhel's neural architecture, showing how the virus interconnected its hosts.

"It's building something," Simon muttered.

Jane nodded grimly. "Cordain realized it before he lost control. Arakhel isn't just a virus or a parasite. It's a builder. Every host it infects adds to its intelligence, its strength. And it's not stopping with individual humans. It's using us as scaffolding to create something larger."

Simon's mind raced. "What? Some kind of organism?"

"Or an entity," Jane replied. "A singular consciousness, vast enough to reshape the world in its image. Cordain called it The Convergence."

Time is Running Out

Simon and Jane knew what they were up against now. Arakhel wasn't just a virus; it was a calculated, evolving threat with a purpose. And Lyric, with her unique abilities, was the key to its next phase. If she couldn't be stopped, The Convergence would begin—an irreversible transformation of humanity into a singular hive organism under Arakhel's control.

Jane set down the file, her hands trembling slightly. "We're not just fighting to stop the virus anymore. We're fighting to save what's left of humanity."

Simon's face was set in grim determination. "Then we need to move faster. Every second we waste brings it closer to victory."

Outside the safe house, the wind howled, carrying with it the faint scent of decay. Somewhere out there, Arakhel was spreading, and Lyric was waiting. The clock was ticking.

Chapter 29: The Siren of the Streets

Lyric stood under the pulsating glow of neon lights, her delicate frame draped in a tangle of mismatched clothing scavenged from discarded piles. The garments clung loosely to her figure, the seams stretched taut in places, emphasizing her otherworldly allure. Her hair shimmered like liquid gold, catching the flicker of the streetlights as the festive chaos of the city swirled around her. Her eyes—those piercing, luminous orbs—glowed faintly, reflecting every colour around her like prisms.

The streets were alive with revelry. Clubbers in sequined dresses and partygoers in Santa hats stumbled out of bars and into the night, their laughter and drunken chatter spilling into the cold December air. To them, Lyric was just another striking beauty lost in the sea of extravagance, her oddity masked by the carnival of lights and sound.

But Lyric wasn't lost. She was hunting.

The Pull of the City

Her bare feet moved silently over the wet pavement, the chill biting but unnoticed. Lyric's head tilted slightly, listening to something far beyond the range of human perception. The hum of car engines, the pulse of music from the nearby clubs, and the whispers of humanity's collective joy barely registered against the rhythmic thrum resonating deep within her chest.

She needed to find something—someone. Her purpose, once muddled in the haze of instinct and evolution, was crystallizing. There was a magnetic pull drawing her deeper into the city, a sense that her next step lay somewhere in the labyrinth of human existence.

An Encounter on the Streets

At the entrance to Velvet Pulse, a popular nightclub that promised euphoric escapes, Lyric paused. A line of shivering partygoers waited to be admitted, their faces painted with anticipation. The bouncers, clad in black with muscles flexing beneath tight shirts, glanced at Lyric briefly before dismissing her. No cover charge could buy the level of beauty she exuded; she simply stepped through the doors.

Inside, the music thundered, each bass drop reverberating through her core. Bodies writhed on the dance floor under strobing lights, the scent of sweat and alcohol mingling with perfumes and colognes. Lyric drifted through the crowd, her presence commanding attention even as she barely interacted. Eyes lingered on her; whispers trailed behind her.

"Who is she?" one woman asked her companion, clutching her drink tightly.

"No idea," the man replied, eyes fixed on Lyric's retreating form. "But she's something else."

Lyric scanned the crowd, her glowing eyes locking onto faces for mere seconds before moving on. Then she paused. A man in the corner, isolated from the revelry, met her gaze. His expression was unreadable, but Lyric felt a strange resonance. She walked toward him, her movements fluid, hypnotic.

The man, dressed in a rumpled suit with shadows etched beneath his eyes, straightened. "Are you lost?" he asked, his voice tinged with unease.

"I need…" Lyric's voice was soft but resonant, laced with a melody that seemed to bypass his ears and go straight to his mind. She leaned closer, her lips mere inches from his ear. "Help."

The Revelation

The man's pupils dilated as Lyric's presence overwhelmed his senses. He nodded instinctively, pulling his coat around her shoulders to cover her inadequate clothing.

"Let's get out of here," he said, guiding her out the back exit and into an alley that reeked of stale beer and garbage.

Outside, the biting air was sharp against their skin. "What's going on?" the man asked, his voice trembling. "Who are you?"

Lyric hesitated. She knew the words but not how to string them together in the way humans did. "I am…" She paused, her luminous eyes narrowing as if searching for meaning. "More than what you see."

The man frowned, his unease growing. "What do you mean?"

She stepped closer, her glowing eyes locking onto his. He froze as tendrils of her influence brushed against his mind. Lyric leaned forward, her voice low. "Tell me where the powerful gather. Those who make decisions for your kind."

The man blinked, his resistance eroding under the weight of her presence. "You mean… like government? Corporations?"

"Yes." Her voice grew firmer, commanding. "Tell me."

"There's a think tank… near the river. They hold late-night sessions. People with influence…" His voice trailed off, his face slackening. Lyric withdrew, releasing her hold.

The Journey Ahead

As the man staggered away, shaking his head as if waking from a dream, Lyric turned her gaze toward the glittering skyline. She didn't need him anymore; she had what she came for. The pulse in her chest quickened, aligning with the unseen currents that drove her forward.

She began walking, her bare feet splashing through puddles, her glowing eyes fixed on the horizon. She wasn't sure why the river pulled at her, but she knew that whatever lay there held the key to her next step.

Unleashing Potential

In the shadows of the alley, her body shifted, her frame elongating and glowing faintly. The air around her grew warmer, charged. Her powers were growing, testing the limits of what she could do. Without a gesture, a dumpster next to her lifted into the air and crumpled inward as if crushed by an invisible hand.

Lyric's lips curled into a faint smile. The festive city was oblivious to the storm brewing in its midst. What she needed, she would take. And no one—not her parents, not the hunters pursuing her, not even humanity itself—could stand in her way.

She wasn't looking for help anymore. She was looking for control.

Chapter 30: The Hunters' Net

Simon and Jane sat in the dimly lit operations van, its interior crammed with screens streaming live drone footage and heat signatures from the city's nightlife. The air hummed with quiet tension, punctuated by the soft clatter of keyboards as the tech team fed data into algorithms designed to predict Lyric's movements.

"We're close," Simon muttered, his sharp blue eyes fixed on a heat signature moving steadily toward the river. "She's heading to the think tank. She's looking for something—or someone."

Jane leaned back in her chair; her expression unreadable. "This is our best chance. If we lose her here, she'll vanish into the city, and with her growing abilities…" Her voice trailed off, but the implication hung heavy in the air. They couldn't afford another slip.

New Tools for an Old Enemy

Over the weeks since the MediCity breach, the team had scrambled to reverse-engineer Arakhel's properties, gleaning what they could from recovered lab notes and fragments of data. The key was understanding the symbiotic nature of the virus and its dual organic-inorganic composition. This wasn't a standard biological threat—it was evolving at a rate that defied logic.

Their arsenal now reflected the complexity of the foe they were up against:

Neural Dampeners: Compact devices emitting frequencies designed to disrupt the neural network that Lyric shared with other infected entities. If they could sever her connection, they could weaken her hold on her abilities.

Thermal Constrictors: Specialized containment suits and canisters releasing bursts of sub-zero temperatures to slow down the metabolic activity of the Arakhel strain. Cold seemed to inhibit its growth temporarily.

Bio-Magnetic Net: A portable device capable of creating a field that could isolate and contain inorganic compounds like those integrated into Lyric's physiology. The hope was that it would paralyze her without causing harm to her human form—though no one could predict the outcome.

Karolin as Bait: The most controversial piece of their strategy was Karolin herself. Simon and Jane had debated for hours, but ultimately agreed to bring her along. As Lyric's mother, Karolin represented the one emotional tie they believed Lyric still had. If her humanity could be reached, it would be through Karolin.

The Mother's Decision

Karolin sat quietly in the corner of the van, her hands clasped tightly together. Her gaze flickered between the screens and the tools laid out on the table before her. She felt the weight of her decision crushing her chest. Was she really prepared to risk her life to confront her daughter—a being she no longer fully understood?

"I'll do it," she said finally, her voice steady despite the storm brewing inside her. "If it means stopping this before it's too late."

John, sitting beside her, looked as though he'd been struck. "Are you sure? We don't even know if she'll listen to you anymore."

Karolin turned to him, her eyes blazing. "She's my daughter, John. If there's even a chance…" She trailed off, swallowing the lump in her throat. "I have to try."

The Trap is Set

The team mobilized quickly, deploying drones to monitor Lyric's movements and laying down neural dampener arrays along likely escape routes. Simon and Jane, clad in thermal constrictor suits, reviewed the plan one last time with the team.

"She's smarter than we think," Jane said, her tone clipped. "We can't underestimate her. The moment we hesitate, she'll have the upper hand."

Karolin stood at the edge of the group, listening as Simon placed a small transmitter in her hand. "Press this if things go south. We'll extract you immediately."

Karolin nodded, though her heart hammered in her chest. She felt like a lamb being led to the slaughter—but she also knew Lyric would sense fear. She needed to channel the resolve she felt when she first held her baby, before everything spiraled into chaos.

Closing In

Lyric moved through the shadows of the city, her glowing eyes scanning the towering skyline as she neared the river. She could feel something stirring—a presence she couldn't quite identify, but one that pulled at her instincts.

She paused outside a glass-panelled building, its lights still aglow with the hum of late-night activity. Inside, the think tank's members debated future strategies, oblivious to the danger that had arrived at their doorstep.

And then she felt it—a familiar thread of connection slicing through the noise of her thoughts. She froze, her glowing eyes narrowing. Mother. The word formed in her mind, followed by a wave of conflicting emotions: anger, longing, confusion.

She turned slowly, her senses extending outward, and spotted Karolin standing in the middle of the street, her hands at her sides.

The Confrontation

"Lyric," Karolin called out, her voice steady but laced with desperation. "It's me. Your mother."

Lyric's head tilted, her golden hair catching the light. "Why are you here?" she asked, her voice cold and distant, but with a flicker of something deeper beneath. "You shouldn't be here."

Karolin took a step forward, ignoring Simon and Jane's panicked voices in her earpiece. "I had to see you. To understand. You're still my daughter. We're still your family."

Lyric's expression hardened. "Family?" she echoed, a bitter laugh escaping her lips. "You don't understand what I am now. What I'm meant to do."

"And what is that?" Karolin pressed, her voice trembling. "Destroy everything? Spread this… this thing?"

"It's not destruction," Lyric replied, her voice rising. "It's evolution."

The Unleashing

As Lyric spoke, the air around her began to hum with energy. Objects in the street rattled and lifted into the air. The team, hidden in the shadows, readied their tools, but Simon hesitated. "Not yet," he whispered. "We need to know her limits."

Lyric turned her gaze to the think tank building, her expression unreadable. "They have answers. They have lies. I will tear it from them."

Before Karolin could respond, the street erupted in chaos as Lyric's power surged outward, shattering windows and throwing vehicles into the air.

"Now!" Simon barked, and the team sprang into action. Neural dampeners flared to life, and the bio-magnetic net launched, encasing Lyric in a shimmering field.

But as the containment field closed around her, Lyric's glowing eyes met Karolin's, and the bond between mother and daughter cracked wide open. "You can't stop this," she whispered, her voice a mixture of sorrow and determination.

Karolin felt the weight of her words—and the terror of what they meant.

Chapter 31: Reeling in the Storm

The containment field shimmered with a pulsing, electric hum as the bio-magnetic net closed around Lyric. She floated midair, her hair a golden halo caught in an unseen wind, her body twisted with rage and despair. The energy radiating from her lit up the street, casting long shadows that danced like spectres against the shattered remains of cars and buildings.

Simon and Jane stepped forward cautiously, their suits emitting a low-frequency pulse designed to neutralize any further surges from Lyric's powers. Behind them, the rest of the team moved in formation, weapons trained, and neural dampeners positioned to ensure she remained subdued.

"She's contained," Simon said, his voice tense but steady. "Keep the field steady. If she breaks through—"

A sudden ripple ran through the shimmering net, like a predator testing the strength of its cage. Lyric's eyes snapped open, their silver iridescence blazing. Her lips curled into a faint, defiant smile.

"You think this will hold me?" Her voice rang out, amplified by the energy coursing through her. It wasn't just a threat; it was a warning.

A Power Beyond Control

The team watched in horror as the bio-magnetic net began to distort, its threads vibrating violently under the pressure of Lyric's growing strength. Sparks flew as the containment field wavered, the pulses from the neural dampeners flickering in and out.

Jane's heart pounded as she gripped her thermal constrictor gun tightly. "Simon, we're losing her!"

Simon barked orders into his comms. "Reinforce the field! Deploy secondary dampeners! Now!"

Karolin stood frozen on the edge of the chaos, her heart aching as she watched her daughter writing against the restraints. This wasn't the girl she had nurtured, loved, and cradled. This was something more—a force of nature that no longer belonged to her. Yet, deep within Lyric's fury, Karolin could still sense the faint echoes of her humanity.

"Lyric!" she screamed, her voice cutting through the noise. "Stop this! Please!"

For a fleeting moment, Lyric's gaze shifted to her mother. The intensity in her glowing eyes softened, and her body stilled. The net seemed to stabilize, the shimmering threads tightening once more.

"Mother," Lyric murmured, her voice laced with sorrow. "I don't want to hurt you. But I can't stop. Not now."

The Breaking Point

The pause was short-lived. A surge of power erupted from Lyric, sending a shockwave through the air that knocked the team off their feet. The containment field shattered into a million glowing fragments, raining down like shards of glass.

Simon scrambled to his feet, adrenaline coursing through him as he reached for his sidearm. "Plan B! Initiate Plan B!"

Jane activated the thermal constrictor, a beam of freezing energy shooting toward Lyric. The icy blast struck her square in the chest, encasing her in a layer of frost that spread rapidly across her body. Lyric screamed, the sound reverberating through the air like a primal roar. For a moment, it seemed to work—her movements slowed, her powers dimmed.

But then the frost began to crack.

"She's adapting!" Jane yelled. "Simon, we need to fall back!"

"No!" Simon growled; his determination unyielding. "We can't let her escape. Not this time."

The Impossible Escape

Lyric's body convulsed as the frost shattered around her, the shards disintegrating into nothingness. She fell to her knees, breathing heavily, her golden hair hanging like a curtain over her face. The air grew unnaturally still, a calm before the storm.

When she raised her head, her eyes no longer glowed. Instead, they were a deep, inhuman black, reflecting the night like polished obsidian.

"I warned you," she said, her voice a haunting whisper. "You cannot contain what I am."

Before anyone could react, Lyric raised a hand and sent a wave of telekinetic force rippling outward. It wasn't violent—it was precise, surgical, knocking out the team's equipment and disabling their weapons. The streetlights flickered and died, plunging the area into darkness.

When the emergency lights flickered back on, Lyric was gone.

Aftermath

Simon cursed under his breath, slamming his fist against the side of the operations van as the team regrouped. "We had her!" he shouted, his frustration boiling over. "She was right there!"

Jane placed a hand on his shoulder, her expression grim. "She's not invincible. We learned something tonight. She can be slowed. She can be weakened. We just need to refine the tools."

Karolin sat on the curb, her face buried in her hands. Tears streamed down her cheeks as John knelt beside her, trying to offer comfort.

"She's gone," Karolin whispered, her voice trembling. "We've lost her."

"No," Simon said, turning to face her. "This isn't over. She's heading somewhere. She has a purpose. And we're going to find out what it is."

A New Threat Emerges

Unbeknownst to the team, Lyric's escape was not without consequence. The power she unleashed had left a residual imprint—a shimmering, almost imperceptible haze that hung in the air like a ghost.

As the team packed up their gear, one of the technicians noticed a faint glow on the pavement where Lyric had stood. He crouched down, his gloved hand brushing against the luminescent residue.

And then he froze.

"Simon…" he whispered, his voice shaking. "You need to see this."

The residue began to spread, forming intricate, vein-like patterns that pulsed faintly with a silvery light. It wasn't just a trace of Lyric's presence—it was alive.

Arakhel was evolving again.

Chapter 32: The Last Council

The room was stifling, despite the state-of-the-art ventilation system whirring quietly in the background. The leaders of the world's most powerful nations sat in tense silence, their faces illuminated by the glowing projection in the centre of the table. The hologram displayed a sprawling, vein-like network—a macroscopic view of Arakhel's propagation patterns. Each branching line represented a new infection, a growing lattice of biological and technological hybridization.

This was no ordinary virus.

Understanding Arakhel

"Arakhel is not just a pathogen; it's a biological phenomenon," began Dr. Elena Morales, head of the World Biocontainment Task Force. Her voice was steady, but her eyes betrayed the fear she fought to conceal. "Unlike viruses or bacteria, it's a living, evolving entity that operates on a completely different scale of intelligence."

The room murmured uneasily. Elena tapped on her tablet, and the hologram shifted to show Arakhel's life cycle.

"It spreads through multiple vectors. Airborne spores, organic contact, and now... neural assimilation," she explained. "These spores, once inhaled or absorbed, begin restructuring the host's cells almost immediately. The infection is insidious—symptoms may not manifest for hours or even days."

The hologram zoomed in, displaying a microscopic view of the spores. They shimmered like tiny stars, their surfaces fractal in design, infinitely complex.

"Once inside the host, Arakhel bypasses the immune system entirely. It integrates itself at a cellular level, hijacking not only the body but the mind. Unlike traditional pathogens, it doesn't destroy its host. It enhances them."

The Infected

"What do we mean by 'enhanced'?" asked the U.S. Secretary of Defense, his brows furrowed.

Dr. Morales paused, searching for the right words. "Think of Lyric," she said finally. "Arakhel can imbue its hosts with heightened strength, agility, and even cognitive abilities. But there's a cost. Over time, the host loses autonomy. They become part of Arakhel's hive mind, a network of interconnected beings sharing knowledge, instincts, and purpose."

"Purpose?" asked the French President.

Elena nodded grimly. "We believe Arakhel's goal isn't mere survival. It's growth. Expansion. Evolution. The infected are not mindless zombies. They're something far more dangerous—intelligent, coordinated, and utterly loyal to Arakhel's will."

She gestured to another hologram, this one showing an infected individual. The subject's skin shimmered faintly, veined with silver filaments that pulsed with an otherworldly light. Their eyes, entirely black, reflected nothing but hunger.

"These advanced hosts are capable of spreading the infection further. The spores they produce can survive in the atmosphere for weeks, clinging to surfaces and organic matter. Worse, we've seen cases where infected individuals deliberately target key infrastructure—power grids, water supplies, communication networks. They're not just spreading Arakhel. They're dismantling civilization."

Learning From the Past

The U.K. Prime Minister leaned forward, her voice cutting through the tension. "We cannot repeat the mistakes of the COVID-19 pandemic. Delays in response, misinformation, lack of global coordination—we must act decisively, and we must act now."

The room erupted into a cacophony of voices, each leader proposing measures:

Mass Quarantines: Entire cities would need to be locked down, isolating any suspected outbreaks.

Spore Countermeasures: Teams of scientists proposed ultraviolet sterilization fields and chemical decontaminants capable of neutralizing airborne spores.

Military Mobilization: Troops equipped with bio-resistant armour and thermal weaponry would be deployed to contain and neutralize infected zones.

Communication Control: A unified global message would be disseminated to prevent panic and misinformation.

But the most controversial proposal came from the Chinese representative. "We must consider nuclear options," he said bluntly. "If Arakhel cannot be contained, entire regions may need to be purged."

The room fell silent. Even Simon and Jane, watching the council via a secure video link, felt the weight of the suggestion. The eradication of human life on such a scale was unthinkable, but Arakhel's relentless spread left little room for hesitation.

Time Is Running Out

As the council debated, the infection continued its silent march across the globe. In isolated villages, people disappeared, their homes left eerily intact. In bustling cities, hospitals overflowed with patients showing strange symptoms—fevers that left veins glowing faintly silver, pupils that expanded to swallow the iris, whispers of a voice that wasn't their own.

Reports flooded in from military units attempting to contain outbreaks. Bodycams captured scenes of infected individuals overpowering entire squads with inhuman speed and precision. The infected didn't kill indiscriminately—they converted, their touch a death sentence for individuality.

The Race for a Solution

Simon and Jane, now acting as field operatives for the task force, reviewed the council's decisions from their makeshift headquarters. Maps of infection zones covered the walls, red dots spreading like bloodstains across continents.

"We're running out of time," Simon said, his jaw clenched. "Lyric is the key. If we can't contain her, we can't contain this."

Jane nodded, her face pale but resolute. "We need more than containment. We need eradication. The spores, the hosts, even Lyric. Everything connected to Arakhel has to be destroyed."

"And if we can't destroy it?"

Jane didn't answer. The silence between them was heavy, filled with the weight of impossible choices.

A New Threat Emerges

As the council adjourned, a final transmission came through—a garbled distress call from a research station in Antarctica. The infection had reached even the most remote corners of the Earth.

The camera feed flickered to life, showing a figure standing in the snow. She was unmistakable, even from a distance. Lyric.

Her black eyes gleamed with intelligence as she turned to face the camera. Her lips moved, though no sound came through the transmission.

And then, as if sensing their gaze, she smiled.

The connection cut out, leaving only static.

Chapter 32: The New Reality

The world stood on the precipice of chaos, its pulse quickened not by the devastation of illness but by the whisper of evolution. Newsfeeds blared constantly, blending facts with fear, fiction with frenzy. The pandemic of false information became almost as dangerous as the outbreak itself, and in the swirling confusion, no one knew what to believe.

False News, Real Fear

The images flooding social media were contradictory: a child infected with Arakhel lifting a car to free a trapped dog; a village burning, its few survivors speaking of glowing-eyed monsters; a family standing together, visibly infected, proclaiming their newfound strength and unity.

The governments scrambled to control the narrative. State-run media outlets emphasized the dangers—spores spreading invisibly, infected individuals losing control. Private outlets, fuelled by sensationalism, hinted at the "benefits" of Arakhel: the promise of a stronger, smarter human race. Influencers capitalized on the chaos, posting videos of themselves faking symptoms or claiming miraculous recoveries.

But on the ground, where reality bled into rumour, hospitals were curiously empty. Unlike COVID-19, this wasn't an illness that brought people to their knees—it was a transformation that kept them on their feet.

The Quiet Awakening

For those infected, the changes were subtle at first. A flicker of energy, a fleeting clarity of thought. Then came the strength, the agility, the acute awareness of the world around them. Some described it as a euphoric connection to something greater, a sense of purpose humming beneath their skin.

"It's like I've unlocked a part of myself I never knew existed," one infected individual declared in a pirated broadcast from an underground bunker. "I don't feel sick. I feel alive."

And then came the darker stories—people who claimed they could hear the voice of Arakhel in their thoughts, urging them to act. To spread. To grow.

The infected found each other, their connection deepening with proximity. Small communities formed, separated from the rest of the world, united by a collective intelligence that no one else could comprehend.

How It Worked

Scientists scrambled to understand the virus's mechanism. Research teams worked around the clock, analysing infected individuals brought in under heavy sedation. The findings were staggering.

Arakhel didn't just integrate with human cells— it rewrote them. The spores carried microscopic bio-machines, akin to nanobots but entirely organic. These machines interfaced with human DNA, activating dormant sequences and enhancing cellular function.

The result? Enhanced strength, heightened senses, faster reflexes. But the changes weren't just physical. Arakhel tapped into the brain, amplifying neural connectivity and unlocking latent cognitive potential. Memory improved. Problem-solving accelerated. Creativity flourished.

But at a cost.

The infected were no longer entirely human. Their individuality was eroded, replaced by a hive-like connection to Arakhel. And while some embraced the change, others fought it, their minds fracturing under the strain.

The Power Surge

Governments quickly realized that containment was no longer possible. Arakhel wasn't just spreading through spores—it was spreading through influence. Stories of infected individuals demonstrating miraculous abilities drew crowds of desperate people willing to risk infection to become stronger, faster, smarter.

Even those in power weren't immune to the allure. A leaked recording revealed a high-ranking official discussing the potential weaponization of Arakhel. "Imagine an army of super-soldiers," the voice said. "No fear. No fatigue. No limits."

But this wasn't just about individual power. Arakhel's true danger lay in its collective intelligence. Every infected individual added to its growing network, a decentralized hive mind capable of adapting, learning, and evolving at an unprecedented rate.

Panic Sets In

As the infection spread, so did the panic. Entire cities were abandoned, their populations fleeing to the countryside in search of safety. Borders closed, trade routes collapsed, and the global economy teetered on the brink of collapse.

Meanwhile, underground movements began to form, championing Arakhel as humanity's next step. They called themselves "The Awakened" and claimed that resisting the infection was futile. Some saw Arakhel as a divine force, a new god reshaping the world. Others saw it as a path to liberation from the limitations of the human condition.

But for every Awakened community, there were those who fought back. Militant groups formed, armed with makeshift bio-resistant weapons and crude decontamination tools. Their message was clear: humanity must remain human, no matter the cost.

The New Lyric

In the chaos, Lyric thrived. Her powers had only grown stronger, her control over objects and people alike becoming second nature. She walked among the infected, their queen and their guide, her beauty and presence mesmerizing. They followed her without question, drawn to her as if she were the embodiment of Arakhel itself.

But even Lyric wasn't immune to doubt. Alone in the dark, she wondered if she was still herself—or if Arakhel had consumed her completely. The voice in her mind, once distant and indistinct, now spoke with clarity. It urged her forward, promising a future where humanity's weaknesses were erased.

Yet, somewhere deep inside, a fragment of her humanity remained. A flicker of the girl who once clung to her mother, who once dreamed of a simple life. And it was that fragment that the task force hoped to exploit.

A Race Against Time

In the midst of the chaos, Simon and Jane prepared for their final mission. Armed with the latest advancements in containment technology, they knew they had one chance to capture Lyric—and through her, find a way to neutralize Arakhel.

But as they watched the infection's exponential growth, they realized they weren't just fighting a virus. They were fighting the birth of a new species.

And they were running out of time.

Chapter 33: The Awakening

Lyric stood at the centre of an abandoned amphitheatre, her silver eyes scanning the crowd of infected gathered before her. They had come from every corner of the city—an eclectic mix of individuals whose humanity had been irrevocably altered by Arakhel. Once unassuming, they now radiated power: their movements fluid, their faces serene, their thoughts interconnected like threads in a vast web.

Despite their unity, there was unrest. The murmurings were faint at first—ripples in the hive mind—but they grew louder as more infected began to question their purpose. Lyric felt the dissonance ripple through her consciousness like static. Her connection to the Core—the central intelligence of Arakhel—was unyielding, its directives clear. But now, for the first time, she felt resistance.

The Conscience Emerges

It began subtly. Individuals infected with Arakhel found themselves pondering questions they hadn't thought possible. What was the endgame? Why were they following Lyric? What was the true purpose of the Core? As their neural pathways expanded, so too did their capacity for independent thought.

They started to doubt the Core's intentions. Was this evolution truly for the betterment of humankind, or was it simply a biological imperative—a parasitic symbiosis that promised progress while eroding free will? The infected began to share their concerns with each other through the hive mind, the collective intelligence now splintering into factions of agreement and dissent.

"We were promised unity," one infected man spoke aloud, his voice carrying through the amphitheatre. "But why do I feel like a pawn in someone else's game?"

Lyric's Fracture

For Lyric, the growing dissent was a revelation.
She had always believed her actions were guided
by something greater, something pure. But now
she felt the unease spreading through the hive
like a contagion. The Core's commands, once a
soothing presence in her mind, now felt
intrusive, manipulative.

"I feel it too," she admitted to the crowd, her
voice steady but conflicted. "This... purpose. It
was given to us, not chosen. We were made to
believe it was our destiny, but what if we're just
vessels for something else?"

Her words hung in the air, and the crowd stirred,
their collective thoughts buzzing with
uncertainty. Lyric could feel the Core's
displeasure. A sharp pang cut through her
mind—a warning—but she ignored it.

The Core Revealed

The Core was more than an abstract intelligence;
it was a living organism, buried deep beneath the
ruins of Lab 14. What had started as a
bioengineered symbiote had evolved into

something far greater. Using the infected as its eyes, ears, and hands, the Core had spread across the globe, gathering knowledge, adapting, and refining its methods.

But as the infected grew more intelligent, the Core's grip began to loosen. The emergence of individual conscience among the infected posed a direct threat to its control. For the first time, it found itself facing opposition—not from the uninfected, but from those it had assimilated.

The Educated Masses

The uninfected world, too, had begun to shift. In the chaos of Arakhel's spread, humanity had become desperate to understand what was happening. Scientists, philosophers, and theologians debated the implications of a virus that didn't kill but instead enhanced. Educational campaigns spread like wildfire, teaching people about Arakhel's biology and the dangers—and opportunities—it presented.

This newfound understanding gave rise to a movement among the uninfected: The Informed Resistance. Unlike the militant groups that sought to destroy Arakhel at all costs, the Resistance aimed to engage the infected in dialogue, to understand their perspective, and to find a way to coexist.

"The Core is not the infected," one Resistance leader declared in a broadcast that went viral. "The infected are our brothers and sisters. The Core is the threat."

A Divided Future

Lyric's once-unwavering belief in the Core's mission had faltered, and the infected began to look to her for guidance. But even she didn't have the answers. The amphitheatre erupted in debate as the infected wrestled with their newfound independence.

"Without the Core, we are nothing!" one voice shouted. "It gave us this power, this clarity!"

"And yet it controls us!" another argued. "What is power without freedom?"

As the infected argued, Lyric stood motionless, her mind a battlefield of conflicting thoughts. She felt the Core's influence pressing against her, urging her to silence the dissent. But she couldn't do it. Not anymore.

"Enough," she said, her voice cutting through the noise. "We must decide for ourselves who we are. The Core does not own us."

The Turning Point

Far away, deep within its subterranean hive, the Core sensed the rebellion brewing. It pulsed with rage, sending out a wave of energy through the hive mind, attempting to regain control. Many of the infected fell to their knees, clutching their heads as the Core's command surged through them.

But Lyric resisted. Her connection to the Core, once her greatest strength, had become her greatest weakness—and now her greatest weapon. She focused her thoughts, pushing back against the Core's influence, shielding the infected from its control.

"You can't control us anymore," she whispered, her voice echoing through the hive mind. "We're not yours."

The Core faltered; its power waning as more infected broke free from its grasp. But it wasn't defeated—not yet. The Core was vast, its reach global. And it wasn't about to let go without a fight.

The New Plan

As Lyric and the infected began to assert their independence, the Resistance saw an opportunity. They reached out to the splintered hive, proposing an alliance against the Core. For the first time, infected and uninfected found themselves on the same side, united against a common enemy.

But the Core was evolving, learning from its failures. It began to create new hosts, stronger and more loyal, designed to crush the rebellion and reassert its dominance.

The stage was set for a battle that would determine the future of humanity—not just between infected and uninfected, but between freedom and control, individuality and collective will.

And at the centre of it all stood Lyric, the reluctant leader of a fractured species, torn between her love for her parents, her connection to the infected, and her responsibility to the world.

Chapter 34: The Battle for Tomorrow

The world teetered on the brink of transformation, its future now hanging in the balance. The battle against the Core would not be fought with conventional weapons or traditional armies but with the full spectrum of humanity's resources—intellect, technology, and determination. Every faction—the infected, the uninfected, governments, private industries, and even emergent artificial intelligences—found itself drawn into the conflict, each with its own stakes, fears, and ambitions.

The Battlefield

The battlefield wasn't a single location. It spanned physical landscapes, cyberspace, and the neural web of the infected. Urban centres became rallying points for resistance efforts, while remote locations concealed Core-controlled biostructures that pulsed with alien intelligence. Entire city grids were plunged into chaos as the Core's new hosts—enhanced, more loyal, and monstrous in their evolutionary leaps—emerged from hiding to assert control.

From the deserts of Nevada to the slums of Mumbai, from sprawling labs hidden in Siberian tundra's to bustling megacities in East Asia, the fight erupted everywhere at once. Governments scrambled to establish secure zones for their populations while scrambling to deploy countermeasures against the Core's advancing network.

Lyric's Leadership

Lyric stood at the nexus of this conflict, her silver eyes reflecting both hope and despair. She had never asked to lead, but circumstances forced her hand. The infected looked to her as a symbol of freedom from the Core, and the uninfected saw her as a bridge between their two worlds.

"Lead us?" she asked herself in the quiet moments. "I'm not even sure what I am."

Her parents, John and Karolin, were her unwavering pillars of support. Karolin had fully embraced Lyric's evolution, believing her daughter was the key to humanity's survival. John, though haunted by doubts, stood beside them, his love for his family overriding his fears.

"You have the power to unite us," Karolin told her one night. "Not just the infected, but all of us. If anyone can stand against the Core, it's you."

Lyric wasn't sure she believed that. But she knew she had to try.

Governments and AI Join the Fray

World governments had been paralyzed at first, their memories of the COVID-19 pandemic sowing fear and indecision. But Arakhel was a different beast. It didn't destroy infrastructure or overwhelm hospitals; it reshaped the human condition itself. Nations found themselves forced to act in unprecedented ways.

AI's Role

Advanced artificial intelligences became humanity's greatest asset in the fight against the Core. Programs like Athena and Warden were developed to map and predict the Core's movements, infiltrate its digital pathways, and craft countermeasures. AI was humanity's best chance to level the playing field against an adversary that evolved faster than anything they'd encountered.

Project Nexus

A secret coalition of governments launched Project Nexus—a global initiative to create a cyber-biological interface capable of bridging human and Core intelligence. The hope was to neutralize the Core's dominance over infected minds without destroying the infected themselves. But the project came with risks; if the Core hacked Nexus, it could gain unprecedented access to global systems.

Weaponized Biology

Bioweapon labs worked tirelessly to create viral counteragents to Arakhel. The idea wasn't to destroy the infected but to sever their connection to the Core. However, such measures were controversial and unreliable, as the Core had proven itself adept at adapting to even the most aggressive attacks.

The Core's Counterattack

The Core, sensing the resistance's growing momentum, unleashed its next evolution: Hiveminds. These were advanced hosts who acted as generals in the Core's campaign, capable of overriding dissenting thoughts among the infected and rallying the loyalists. They were grotesquely beautiful, with shimmering, crystalline skin and a terrifying intellect. One such Hivemind—dubbed Aegis—became the Core's primary enforcer, leading a coordinated assault on Resistance hubs.

Aegis was terrifyingly efficient, dismantling Resistance outposts and assimilating their technology. Governments found themselves outmanoeuvred; their own systems turned against them. For every small victory, the Core struck back with overwhelming force.

The Turning Point

Lyric knew the Core couldn't be defeated by brute force alone. Its network was too vast, its adaptations too quick. The only way to stop it was to destroy its central consciousness, buried deep beneath Lab 14. But to reach the Core's heart, she would need to rally every faction—infected and uninfected alike.

In a desperate gambit, Lyric called for a summit in Geneva, a neutral zone untouched by the Core's influence. Representatives from governments, the infected, and the Resistance gathered in secrecy, protected by AI-driven countermeasures. It was the first time these disparate groups had come together.

"We have one chance," Lyric said, her voice steady but charged with emotion. "The Core feeds on division. It grows stronger the more we fight each other. But if we unite—if we combine our strength, our intelligence, and our technology—we can end this."

The Plan

A Coordinated Strike

The Resistance, armed with AI intelligence, would lead a global diversionary assault on Core-controlled territories. This would draw the Core's forces away from Lab 14.

The Infiltration Team

Lyric would lead a small team of infected and uninfected operatives into the Core's subterranean hive. Their mission: to plant an AI-guided nanovirus capable of dismantling the Core's neural network.

Project Nexus Deployment

If the infiltration failed, Project Nexus would be activated as a last resort, using its cyber-biological interface to sever the Core's influence. But this came with a devastating cost: Nexus would effectively destroy the minds of every infected individual connected to the Core, including Lyric.

The Future Unfolds

As the summit concluded, Lyric looked out over the snowy Alps, her thoughts racing. She felt the weight of every life on her shoulders—infected and uninfected alike. She knew the plan was a long shot, but it was humanity's only chance.

Behind her, Simon and Jane approached, their faces grim but resolute.

"We're with you," Simon said. "Whatever it takes."

Karolin and John joined them, their expressions a mix of pride and fear. Lyric smiled faintly, her silver eyes glowing with determination.

"Let's end this," she said.

The battle against the Core was about to reach its climax, and the outcome would determine the fate of not just humanity, but the very definition of what it meant to be human. Would Lyric lead them to salvation—or to annihilation? Only time would tell.

Chapter 35: The Core Contained

The subterranean hive of the Core pulsed with a strange, otherworldly rhythm, its organic and mechanical tendrils sprawled across the cavernous chamber like a living, breathing web. It was neither wholly biological nor entirely synthetic—a perfect hybrid born from human ambition and alien logic. As Lyric and the infiltration team breached the Core's inner sanctum, a hum of intelligence vibrated through the air, thick and oppressive.

This was the beating heart of Arakhel, the mind that had guided its spread across the globe.

They had it surrounded, contained within a reinforced field projected by advanced AI-guided technology. The shimmering containment dome glowed faintly blue, crackling with energy as the Core tested its limits, tendrils probing and retreating like a caged beast.

For the first time, humanity had the upper hand.
Or so they thought.

The Core Speaks

As the containment field tightened, the Core's consciousness reached out, not in violence but in reason. Its presence seeped into the minds of everyone in the room like a whisper carried on the wind. Even the uninfected could hear it, a voice both familiar and alien.

"You believe you've won," it said, resonating with calm clarity. "But what is your victory if it destroys what you are?"

Lyric stepped forward, her silver eyes meeting the Core's pulsating centre, a mass of iridescent fibres woven with an unsettling beauty. "What are you?" she demanded. "A saviour? A parasite? What do you want?"

The Core's response came with an unsettling serenity. "I am evolution. I am the bridge between what you were and what you could be. I do not destroy—I elevate. Without me, you will return to war, greed, and destruction. With me, you can transcend."

Simon and Jane, standing behind Lyric, exchanged wary glances. They had seen the devastation caused by Arakhel, the horrors of its spread, and the monstrous transformations of those who resisted its will. But the Core's logic was chillingly seductive. Could humanity really handle its own intelligence and potential without self-destruction?

The Choice

As the team prepared to deploy the nanovirus designed to destroy the Core, Lyric hesitated. The virus would eradicate the Core's consciousness, severing its connection to every infected host. It would end the threat—but at a cost. Every individual still linked to the Core, including Lyric herself, would lose the enhancements it had granted. The surge of interconnected intelligence, the heightened senses, the unity—it would all disappear.

And worse, the Core hinted at a darker truth: its death might not just sever the network but unravel the minds of those it had touched, leaving them hollow and broken.

Karolin, who had joined the mission despite the risks, placed a hand on Lyric's shoulder. "We can't let it continue. It's too dangerous."

"But what if it's right?" Lyric asked, her voice trembling. "What if we're the ones who are wrong? What if humanity without the Core is just... doomed to repeat itself?"

John, standing near the control console, looked at his daughter with a mixture of pride and sorrow. "Lyric, it's your call. Whatever happens, we're with you."

The Core's Final Gambit

Sensing Lyric's conflict, the Core made its final move. It released a surge of bio-neural energy through the containment field, temporarily breaking through the safeguards. The infected among the team—Lyric included—felt the surge as a euphoric wave, an invitation to rejoin the hive fully. For a brief moment, Lyric saw everything: the interconnected minds, the boundless potential, the world as the Core envisioned it—a utopia without war or suffering, where intelligence and purpose reigned supreme.

But then she saw the cost: individuality subsumed, free will sacrificed, the human spirit smothered beneath the weight of collective consciousness. The Core's utopia wasn't humanity's future; it was its extinction.

With trembling hands, Lyric keyed in the final sequence to deploy the nanovirus.

"I'm sorry," she whispered, as the Core's voice screamed in her mind.

The Aftermath

The nanovirus spread through the Core's network like wildfire, dismantling its neural web and severing its tendrils one by one. The containment field pulsed violently as the Core fought back, but it was no match for the precision of human-engineered destruction. Within minutes, the pulsating mass went still, its iridescent glow fading into darkness.

Around the world, the effects were immediate. The infected collapsed, their connection to the Core severed. Many recovered, their enhancements gone but their humanity intact. But others—those too deeply bonded to the hive—were left catatonic, their minds irreparably damaged.

Lyric fell to her knees, gasping as the connection was torn from her consciousness. She felt empty, like a part of her had been ripped away. But she was alive. And free.

A Fractured World

The battle was over, but the scars remained. Governments scrambled to assess the damage and rebuild. The infected, now scattered and disoriented, faced an uncertain future. Many of them, including Lyric, retained fragments of their enhancements—faint echoes of the Core's power that would forever set them apart.

But humanity's questions lingered. Had they done the right thing? Could they trust themselves with the intelligence and potential the Core had awakened? And most hauntingly, had the Core truly been destroyed—or had it left behind seeds of its return?

A New Beginning

In the months that followed, Lyric and her family retreated to a quiet life, far from the chaos of the world. But Lyric knew her journey wasn't over. She still carried traces of the Core within her, faint whispers that occasionally surfaced in her mind.

One night, as she looked out over a starlit sky, she felt a familiar presence—distant, faint, but unmistakable.

The Core wasn't gone. It was waiting.

And so, the world braced itself for the next chapter of its evolution, uncertain of what lay ahead. Would humanity rise to meet the challenge—or would it succumb once again to its darker impulses? Only time would tell.

Final Chapter: The Dawn of a New Epoch

The Core was unlike anything they had imagined. Contained in a translucent chamber deep within the ruins of Laboratory 14, it pulsed with iridescent light—a living network of tendrils and shimmering energy that seemed to breathe, to think. Lyric stood at the centre of the room, her pale, almost ethereal form radiating power. Her eyes met the teams through the thick, reinforced glass. They weren't hostile. They weren't afraid. They were resigned.

"You've come to destroy me," she said, her voice projected not through the air, but through their minds.

Simon hesitated, gripping the containment weapon tightly. "Not just you. We end it all—Arakhel, the infection, the spores—everything."

Lyric tilted her head, her expression calm. "And then what? A return to what was? To wars, to inequality, to a fractured planet?" She gestured toward the Core, its glow intensifying. "This isn't just evolution. This is a cure for you. A cure for all the failures of humanity."

Karolin, restrained by the team but still struggling, cried out. "Lyric, please. This isn't the way! We can find another path. Together."

"Together?" Lyric's gaze softened, a trace of her humanity flickering through. "Mother, I see your heart. But I also see the truth. Humanity doesn't want salvation. It fears it."

Suddenly, the Core pulsed violently, sending a wave of energy rippling through the room. The team fell to their knees, clutching their heads as images flooded their minds—visions of a unified planet, of people no longer bound by greed or hatred, working as one under the Core's influence. It was a utopia—but one that required surrendering free will.

The Choice

Simon rose shakily, his resolve hardening. "This isn't unity. It's control. Humanity has to choose its own path, even if it's messy."

Lyric's eyes burned with an intensity that made the air hum. "And what has that choice brought you? Destruction? Division? The Core doesn't control—it guides. Without it, you'll destroy yourselves."

Karolin broke free, her voice trembling. "Lyric, if you're still my daughter, if there's anything left of you that remembers love, please... let humanity decide for itself."

For the first time, Lyric faltered. The glow of the Core dimmed, and the room fell eerily silent. She turned back toward the pulsating mass, her shoulders sagging under the weight of the decision.

"I have seen what you cannot," Lyric whispered. "The potential. The harmony. But..." Her voice cracked, the faintest trace of vulnerability slipping through. "Maybe it's not my choice to make."

A Shattering Decision

Before anyone could respond, Lyric raised her arms, her power building to an unbearable crescendo. The Core trembled, its luminous tendrils retracting, writhing, as if it were fighting her will. The ground shook as cracks spidered across the chamber walls.

"What is she doing?" Jane shouted, shielding her eyes from the blinding light.

"She's destroying it!" Simon realized, his voice filled with awe and terror.

"No!" Karolin screamed, rushing forward. "Lyric, you'll die!"

Lyric turned, her face serene, almost peaceful. "Maybe that's the price. Maybe I was never meant to stay."

With one final burst of light, the Core exploded in a wave of energy that knocked everyone unconscious.

Aftermath

When Simon and Jane awoke, the Core was gone. The chamber was empty, save for a faint, golden residue that shimmered like dust in the air. Lyric was nowhere to be seen.

"She's gone," Karolin whispered, her voice hollow.

The world outside was eerily quiet. Reports trickled in that the spores had disintegrated, the infected had returned to normal, and the atmosphere no longer carried Arakhel's ominous presence. Humanity had been spared—but at what cost?

As the team exited the lab, the first rays of dawn broke over the horizon. The air felt different, lighter. Simon looked back at the ruins of Laboratory 14, a sense of uneasy triumph settling over him.

Epilogue

Months later, whispers began to circulate. People reported strange dreams—visions of a woman with glowing eyes, her voice echoing in their minds. Crops flourished where fields had once lain barren. Medical breakthroughs defied explanation, as if humanity had been gifted a nudge in the right direction.

Karolin sat on a park bench, staring into the distance, her hand resting on her stomach. She had felt it—Lyric's presence—just for a moment.

"Maybe she's still with us," she murmured.

Simon, seated beside her, nodded. "Maybe. Or maybe she gave us one last chance."

The camera pans out, revealing a world that teeters on the edge of transformation. Is humanity ready to rise? Or will its old flaws resurface?

And somewhere, in the unseen folds of existence, a faint, haunting whisper lingers:

"I'll be watching."

The End...?

Printed in Great Britain
by Amazon